CHILDREN AND LUNATICS

CHILDREN AND LUNATICS

a novel

Megan McNamer

Black
Lawrence
Press

Black
Lawrence
Press

www.blacklawrence.com

Executive Editor: Diane Goettel
Book and cover design: Amy Freels

Published 2016 by Black Lawrence Press.
Printed in the United States.

From *Owl Moon* by Jane Yolen, copyright © 1987 by Jane Yolen. Used by permission of Philomel, an imprint of Penguin Young Readers Group, a division of Penguin Random House LLC.

The quote in Section V. (The River) comes from *In the River Sweet* by Patricia Henley, originally published by Anchor Books and used with permission from Penguin Random House,

For John, Patrick, and Willy

Children and lunatics cut the Gordian knot which
the poet spends his life patiently trying to untie.
—Jean Cocteau

CONTENTS

I.

THE MOON

I.

She was beginning to be known.

"I saw you," they said. "I saw you on California Street, on the river path, on Broadway, on the steel steps going down. I saw you downtown."

They spoke with their eyes.

"I saw you walking."

She could change her route or the time of day. Then different people would see her, and they would comment, the words piling up, coming from all directions.

"I saw you at the stoplight by the post office. I saw you going into Macy's. I saw you at the bus station. I saw you on the footpath. I saw you leaving the restaurant."

Even if she wore a disguise, sunglasses, a big floppy hat, a baseball cap, a hooded jacket.

They saw her and their eyes made comment.

~

She walked in all kinds of weather and every season of the year. She walked in the middle days of April when tulips stood lonely and disconsolate under the leaden sky, the temperatures remaining unseasonably cold, the people in the restaurant complaining that they were tired of their winter clothes. She dressed warmly so that she didn't fall into bleakness the first few blocks, the leaves on the trees begrudging in their small display, the sky without color. She carried one of her many satchels, so that she could shed layers as the world improved, stuff them away and continue on, stride unbroken.

She walked in the summertime at high noon, hiding under a straw hat with a leather string tie. She walked in a mission town in Mexico in another century. She walked in the fall, her favorite time, when the afternoon glow transformed the world into a lamp-lit room, a chapel with stained glass, the ceiling painted blue. She walked in winter, hearing her feet, anticipating each moist and gravely footfall.

She walked and walked and walked, and people noticed. Their eyes spoke.

"I saw you."

"I saw you walking."

~

On the left for one block, on the right for the next, she could possibly live in every third house. She tried not to look too far ahead, that would spoil it. Every third house. She knew all the houses along her regular walks, but choosing every third house, first left then right, made the order of appearance irregular, hence unpredictable, a surprise, a kind of prize. Her house. Her lucky number.

A bland, sad house with no shrubs or plantings whatsoever. She would put bright plastic flowers in the scattered pots on the empty cement patio. She would place a chair next to a pot. She would hang a straw hat on a nail on the patio wall. The chair would be secure and sturdy, with arms.

A low-roofed house, practically a shed, with one window cracked. Set far back from the sidewalk, the lawn a mass of weeds, the little house needing paint. Maybe the dwelling place of a wrinkled little man with a bit of garden out back. A forgotten gnome. She would look at this small house and hear wind chimes from across the street, sounding one tone, then another, higher . . . then silence . . . then the first tone again, the air barely stirring. And she would think: It is Wednesday afternoon. It is Wednesday afternoon for everyone, all across the town.

Here was a beautiful, well-kept house with a wide front porch. Hanging planters with late-blooming geraniums and a slatted swing and a sign with curling, wood-burned letters: The Albee's. Spacious and shaded, and inside there would surely be a television and a piano against the wall and books. She wondered about the apostrophe. It likely was a mistaken way to indicate more than one. Certainly, there would be more than one Albee in such a nice, big, shingled bungalow. The apostrophe might also indicate possession. This house belongs to the Albees. But it should come at the very end, then, the apostrophe. This is the Albees' house. This is the Albees'.

It bothered her that the Albees would put up that incorrect sign. But maybe there was, after all, only one of them. The Albee. The Albee's. This is his house.

~

The wide-brimmed hats numbered thirteen, the baseball caps twelve. There were six woolen berets in different colors and three bucket hats, which she didn't wear because they looked like buckets. If she were to have hair to her chin and if it were to be thick and chestnut brown, she would wear a bucket hat. But she wasn't to have that kind of hair, not now, not ever, not in this life. She was to have wispy short hair. She tried to make it a warm Chestnut Brown or a cool Ash or a soft Honey. But it was variously a dark, flat brown that was almost black, as if it had been colored by a permanent marker, or it was an oddly tinged gray, an oil slick in a rain puddle.

She often wore one of the woolen berets to her Wednesdays, to First Wednesday and to all the other Wednesdays. In fall she wore dark green or, this year, a new, taffy-colored pink. In winter she wore black or dark brown, in spring and summer she wore cream or pale gray. Unless it was very hot, in the high nineties, woolen berets did not seem to provide occasion for comment. Once, though, a young woman on the street offered her a white linen beret, right from her own blonde head. But it didn't lay right or feel substantial.

Although she loved them the most and had many, she only wore the wide-brimmed hats when she was planning to walk at a steady clip and—apparent to any observer—not intending to stop anytime soon, if at all. When it was necessary to pause on a street corner to wait for a light, or when she positioned herself at a SMARTbUS stop, the wide-brimmed hats were likely to provoke looks, possibly remarks, as if she were trying to be fancy. In fact, she was traveling incognito. When she wore her wide-brimmed hats she felt that she joined a vast, timeless, faceless coterie of sojourners. The sun beat down on her hat from on high, but she existed within the rim, a secret, shaded area.

Baseball caps were good. She might be a lined and haggard older woman, or she might not. She was trim, from all the walking. When she saw herself in the storefront windows, when the sun was bright and her face was shadowed, she might be a younger person, or even a boy.

Mexico, Italy, the Eastern seaboard of the United States. She walked down many different streets. Baltimore, Maryland at the Turn of the Century. She walked through pages of old magazines, distributed for free on the table in the foyer of the public library. A high mountain village in Nicaragua, a windswept bluff in Mongolia, the ancient civilization of Angkor, collapsed.

Are We Alone?

On a glossy cover was a picture of a pockmarked moon.

Searching the Heavens for Another Earth.

~

2.

First Wednesdays meant the first Wednesday of every month. It didn't mean first Wednesdays and then something else. It was an arbitrary day to go to the restaurant and have a bargain lunch, whoever wanted to. There were signs and reminders about it here and there, in the library foyer, at the SMARTbUS terminal. The cost was two dollars for any of the lunch combos on the menu. Two dollars from eleven a.m. to one p.m. and the rest of the usual charge ($4.50 and upwards) the restaurant donated out of its own funds to nonprofit businesses that supported causes. Secret Treasure, Bargain Box, Goodwill, the Food Bank, they all were beneficiaries of First Wednesdays. As were the restaurant patrons themselves, on those particular days.

She always ordered the soup and salad combo. It came with a basket of bread and little pats of butter and packets of jam. She used one packet of jam and put one packet in her pocket. She drank water, the drinks being extra. The salad might be garden green or pasta. The pasta was macaroni. She always had the pasta salad because the garden green salad was not chopped or shredded very finely, it was a pile of large lettuce leaves that invariably drooped out around the edges of most people's mouths, at least initially, upon the first bite. The cold macaroni could be secreted away quickly, tucked out of sight.

From her own door to the door of the restaurant, walking straight, no stopping, took eleven minutes. It might take twelve or thirteen minutes if the light was wrong at the corner by the post office. After the end of her block there were no houses on the way to the restaurant, just the federal building, the post office, some business offices, a few shops. She kept her eyes straight ahead and took note of no potential abodes.

It took anywhere from eight to ten small bites to eat the pasta salad. She kept her hat on while she ate. She sat alone at the table for two in the corner. It took anywhere from twenty-five to thirty-five minutes, the whole thing, the lunch. And then she was done.

Back inside her rooms, the yellow comforter was folded neatly at the foot of the bed. The *Welcome* mat was two inches from the door frame and centered exactly. Outside in the dim hallway, her key lay secret behind the radiator, waiting for her return.

~

Coming home from the restaurant, she walked a big loop. First she continued on down Main Street and entered Macy's, walking past the cosmetics counter, where she squirted perfume samples on her wrists and neck and clothing. The counter lady's eyes looked at her, but she did not look back. She left by the bank street door, then, and waited for the *Walk* signal at the intersection, then went over Monroe Bridge and carefully descended the steep, steel steps to the riverfront walking path. Sometimes she stopped in at LauraLee's Bakery and had a free sample. Or she went into Bitterroot Herbs and smelled the aromatherapy oil heating in its small dish and examined wooden massage implements, as if thinking to buy one. She had choices. She could choose to go into LauraLee's Bakery or into Bitterroot Herbs. If the day was clear, then she did. If the clouds were high. She examined the sky. Each day when she awoke, she looked for the faceless morning moon ushering the fate of the day.

The steep, steel steps at the end of the bridge led to the walking path at the side of the river. She headed west on the path, ignoring the college joggers, and the young women with their big dogs and the mothers and occasional fathers pushing toddlers in needle-nosed strollers that looked like narrow, cozy wheelbarrows, the solemn-faced child some kind of produce. She walked on the river path for about half a mile, and then, some days, she turned left and wended her way up California Street, sticking close to the edge, since there were no sidewalks, and fast cars with reckless drivers sometimes came around that blind corner, taking a shortcut from one busy street to another. She walked along junkyards and weeds up California Street until she came to the Bargain Box, the Catholic charity thrift shop next to the Sister Agatha Shea Sports Center and adjacent playing fields.

She thought about those words, "reckless drivers." The word: "reckless." NEGLIGENT. *Reck*—worry, care, matter; to care for, regard; to matter to, concern. *Reckless*. Without concern.

~

Some days, after heading west on the walking path, she turned to the right, back toward the river, and she walked until she came to the foot bridge that allowed access back to the other side. After the foot bridge there was a short section of trail paved to accommodate motorized wheelchairs captained by odd-bodied inhabitants of a nearby group home. This trail abutted a youth home, too, where at-risk youths lived. One side of the river was for the general citizenry, joggers and bicyclists and strollers, and middle-aged women in pairs, wearing pedometers. This other side of the river had not yet been improved. She could see the at-risk youths' stuffed animals and other jumbled objects in the windows, but she never saw the youths themselves. The grass around their home was thick and green and untrammeled.

Beyond the youth home the paved trail abruptly ended in thick river brush. Any determined pedestrian had to continue down a graveled alleyway that abutted the back doors of a derelict motel. She rarely saw a motorized wheelchair in this corridor; the ride was bumpy and the eventual crossing on Broadway was dangerous. She might see a derelict standing in a doorway, the gloomy scene within one of casual despair, the unmade bed and random possessions strewn across the floor seeming permanently provisional.

The graveled alleyway ended at a section of Broadway that was a no man's land for anyone not in a car. Traffic here zoomed past in waves, exceeding the 30 mph limit, shooting from downtown to the big box stores on the edge of town and to the airport. There was nothing much to stop for here and little to see except more river on the left, and ancient, family businesses on the right. Eastside Door. Custom West Glass. A-Z Autobody. Rowdy's Roost, a faded steakhouse casino with two hand-scrawled signs propped against the window: "ATM Inside" and "Expresso," the second tipped and sliding down, half out of view.

Secret Treasure was directly across from the derelict motel. It supported the YWCA's Battered Women's Shelter (itself in a secret location) by selling for pennies the cast-off clothing and housewares of wealthy ladies.

She thought about the wealthy ladies. Rich and settled and organized and safe. Unbattered. Ticking sprinklers on the lawn and patio furniture that was as nice as any inside furniture, coordinated and padded. Iced tea on hot afternoons. Plug-in air fresheners.

Memo pads and pencils next to the phones, and the comforters folded just so.

She told herself that she would take the long loop if the weather was indicative, the sky just right. In actual fact she took the long loop home every Wednesday, with no deviation. And when she reached California Street, depending on the previous trip, she turned either to the left or to the right. And then she was rewarded by either the Bargain Box or Secret Treasure after her long trek, after braving the college joggers and the babies in strollers on the river path, the reckless drivers on California street, the lumpish bodies in humming wheelchairs crossing the foot bridge, the invisible at-risk youth and the despairing derelicts, who invariably emitted a friendly "howdy," swaying slightly in their doorways and proffering gappy grins or comments on the clouds.

After that the neighborhoods were residential again, with potential places to live, every third house.

~

3.

In her rooms (the yellow comforter folded neatly at the foot of the bed, the *Welcome* mat exactly two inches from the door, the key now placed in its china saucer on the shelf), she imagined she should feel sobered and sad, thinking of the stuffed animals in the windows of the youth home, and remembering the smells of ashtrays and ancient cooking from the seedy motel, and thinking of the battered women. But instead she almost always felt a low thrum of pleasure deep inside her chest as she filled the tea kettle, a tiny bit of secret glee, because she usually had found a good bargain or secret treasure—a soft cardigan in her favorite red, a little purse with a seashell clasp. She paid her one, two, or three dollars and brought her item home and felt the same happy satisfaction she had felt whenever as a child she had found a plastic egg with a winning number at the Kiwanis Club Easter egg hunt at Riverside Park. A movie pass, a free drink with purchase of a hamburger, the prize specifics or transactional value didn't matter that much. What mattered was finding the egg with the number, in among all the empty others.

She hung a new sweater with her many other sweaters, according to color and type—cardigans together, pullovers together, reds, blacks, blues—sometimes sacrificing a lesser version in order to make room, stuffing the reject into a sack in the back of the closet, a sack that eventually would be tucked discretely behind an alley garbage can somewhere distant. If a newly-acquired sweater carried a faint aroma of some other human she stood still and held it close to her nose and smelled it.

She thought about the person, the lady who had donated the item. She was comfortably well-off, this person who had grown tired of her red sweater, or the purse with the seashell clasp. She sat in her freshly-painted house, secure, a stuffed chicken in the oven and matching furniture in the living room and books on their shelves and mail on a tray in the hall and a magnet on the refrigerator holding the week's shopping list. There was a set of encyclopedias in the bookshelf and a dictionary on its own stand and a globe of the world. There were pictures on the wall, family photos, people lined up at weddings, children in sets of two, clustered close, the older girl's hand on the smaller boy's shoulder. And there was a television encased in wood, and plants, and many lamps with shades that glowed red and yellow. There were candles, slender and tall or thick and squat, carefully unused, candles just for show, next to the bouquets of cloth flowers. And there were many other items lined up inside the cupboards, closets, and drawers.

This person, the wealthy lady, drove to Secret Treasure in her big car to drop off her donation. Then she drove on to the large stores on the edge of town to buy more items. And then she had coffee with a friend, her legs crossed and her coat slung over a chair. She stayed as long as she liked. And then she returned home, swinging the big car off the street and up the driveway as the garage door opened in welcome.

Sometimes she thought about this person all the rest of the afternoon until it was time to pull the shade in her tiny foyer and turn on the rose lamp.

~

4.

She sat in her rocker in the evenings and rocked. She practiced her spelling. She might award herself a new purse as a prize, a prize for correct spelling. She chose a slip from her word slip box, glanced at the word she had written, then looked straight ahead and spelled it out loud, giving its short definition, perhaps a sample sentence. Appearance (n.) semblance, show. *The man in the moon is only an ~.* She was always correct. She put the spelling word in the new purse and put the new purse on the purse shelf, making necessary adjustments. If she was forced to relinquish a purse to make room, she looked again at the word, the word in that particular purse, before relinquishing it, too. Abandon (v.) throw out. Desert. FORSAKE. *~ the children to fate.*

~

5.

It happened on a bus day. Occasionally she gave herself a bus day, when she would get on a SMARTbUS at the downtown terminal—whichever bus was first to arrive, no matter the number or destination—and just ride. She tried not to look at the number, because she generally knew which numbers went where. She tried to make it a surprise.

The Number Five was her favorite. (Only a few times in her experience had it not been first to arrive.) It went up Butler Creek Crossing, winding its way in a leisurely fashion through all the modern houses after the initial fast sail up Butler Creek Drive. The Number Five on a weekday was as empty as the streets. The driver knew her, but she pretended not to know him, so he pretended not to know her. She knew he knew her because he had tried to strike up a conversation once or twice when it was just the two of them. He had commented on her hat. After that she sat farther back and kept her gaze out the window.

She picked a number. She found it in the free news weekly. At the bus terminal she would pick up a paper and leaf through it until she found the number. "Three School Board Vacancies To Be Filled." No. It had to be larger than five. "Ten Ways to Make Halloween 'Spook-tacular'." No. Not "larger-than" enough. "U.S. Military Death Toll Approaching 2,000." No. It had to be less than one hundred. "Fifty-Five Alive: Driving Class Directed at Seniors." Okay.

After the bus passed Butler School she counted to the number at an even tempo. Not so slow as one Mississippi, two Mississippi. She used "aw-loo" instead, the suffix her little brother Eddy would hang on numbers, names, and some nouns. *Mama aw-loo*, he said, at age three. *Sissy aw-loo.* He said, *Santa aw-loo* and *Bunny aw-loo* and *Pinocchio aw-loo.* He said, *I am four aw-loo, five aw-loo.* It was his way of affixing things to the world, keeping them in place. *God aw-loo*, he even said that.

At Halloween Eddy put on the hard-plastic battered Casper the Ghost mask, his breath rasping through the cracks and nose hole, his face like a moon. *Casper aw-loo*, he said with a muffled, buried voice, cocking his stiff smile this way and that.

When she reached the given number (*fifty-five aw-loo*) she pulled the bell, gathered up her satchel, and prepared to get off. The bus glided to a wholly unexpected spot, and she descended, the driver watching her. The bus left with a hiss, the driver's eyes turned back to the road. The quiet, curving street was lined with smooth lawns and sporadic sidewalks. She began to walk, purposefully, head up, satchel tucked under her arm. Eyes open and fixed. She began, again, to count. She counted to half the previous number, rounding to the next highest (*twenty-eight aw-loo*), and when she reached that number she stopped and looked at the house, her house, the house that might be home.

One day it was a two-story house with a sun porch. Another time it was a white painted brick house with a columned front porch and a stone bench. Each time, just looking had the feel of going, going in, she heard an imaginary bell, a signal, *cross the line, careful, proceed, step through . . .*

There were high cirrus clouds on this particular day, long wisps against the palest blue. A faint breeze. A hint of smoke, still lingering from the forest fires of the summer. It was on the cusp, the sky, the air, the day. It was on a fulcrum, balanced between all that had happened and what was yet to come.

After acknowledging her house (two-story stucco, shaded, with half a fence out front and lumber tossed here and there on the lawn, as if more building were in progress), she walked up the angled sidewalk that led to the front door under an archway flanked by bushes. The porch was made from stones. A small brass dog stood next to a bristled mat. A collar hung around the dog's neck. It said "Attack Dachshund." The bell made a chiming sound when she pushed it, and a delayed summons emitted from deep within.

She listened to the chime and to a plane that droned in the sky, far overhead, and to a distant call of a train. She could feel her heart beating. It made her entire body move, slightly, like a tree stirred by a breeze. She pressed the black button again, and heard the chime a second later, and she waited. The jet's monotone receded into silence. The train remained, its presence a rhythmic thrum. Brown flowers in a pot moved just perceptibly in the late autumn air. She turned the knob and gently pushed. The door swung open and let her in.

~

6.

The little dog barked frantically, running in circles. She took a step into the dim foyer and the dog neatly nipped her ankle then flipped over nearly backward in a rebound of nerves and fury. She stood perfectly still as the gyrating creature barked and ran its circles and performed its near flips. Suddenly it stopped on a dime and marched stiffly, toenails clicking, over to the end of the tiled hallway where it flopped its hindquarters and little belly down on the smooth floor.

Silence. She waited, next to the door. No other sounds came from the house, only the refrigerator in the kitchen whirring into cooling mode, a rustle of ice from the ice maker. She moved her hand from her side a few inches into the air, slowly, experimentally. The dog sat up straight, panting, its wet eyes small dots of perplexed emotion.

To her right was the thick green carpet of the living room, like a meadow floor. She pushed the door back into place and moved slowly into the house. She stepped onto the carpet. The dog lay its chin on the hall tiles and watched her and quivered. She took two more steps, until she was just outside the dog's sight. She stopped and listened. The dog's breathing came in jerky pants. It was listening, too. She inched toward a high-backed chair upholstered in a mauve and green scene of horses, hunters, and hounds. Easing down, she held her own breath. She relaxed into the chair, enfolded in its arms.

A clock on the mantel emitted a small grinding noise and then chimed the half-hour. She looked out the window at a weeping birch's slow sashay, a few of its leaves fluttering free, and she looked at the sunlight and shadows on the carpet, moving in patterns like clouds or smoke.

A silver packet of matches nestled in a small clear dish next to a white-wicked candle. Eddy used to call them people. Blackened matches were bodies, fallen heroes, their lingering ghosts short-lived. Burning matches were kings and soldiers, their heads aflame with gold. *Army aw-loo*, said Eddy, flinging the matches.

Magazines on the table were arranged in a fan. *Time, Self, Get Simple, U.S. News and World Report. Globe and Cosmos, The New Millennium—A Special Issue.*

Whatever You Thought, the cover said, *Think Again*.

The fire was the battle and it always grew.

~

II.

THE TRAIN

7.

The carpet had to go, *oh* my god. Puke green, it made you want to weep. It never had recovered from Clark's early puppy days and then his middle-aged days and now his senile days. Whenever she had visitors she said, "The carpet's going, don't worry." She might add, "And the horse-n-dog chair. Dirk's mom." She referenced the hunting hound chair and the mother-in-law who had bequeathed it as if she and Dirk and their possessions were in the public domain of concern to near strangers. She heard herself doing this, heard herself say *stop*, heard herself keep on going. Well, what do you do, when people just stand there?

She gave them a tour of the house. Even if it was just a parent pickup she'd yell down to Sammy in the basement that his friend whoever's mom was here, and then she'd put Clark in the kitchen behind his doggy gate and give the mom a tour of the house. The mom always said, "Oh. Okay . . ." when proffered the offer to tour the house. Then it was upstairs to the bedrooms, her and Dirk's room—with what Dirk called the "football size bed," meaning football field-sized—and Sammy's room, with the empty turtle tank under the window and the fuzzy King Kong footprint rug from Walmart, pretty ratty now, and the Korn posters, a rock band, weird, puppet-like creatures with their mouths sewn shut.

She'd show the touring parent the favorable cosmetic lighting in the master bathroom and the halogen lighting in the second upstairs bathroom and the Art Deco sconces in the hallway. She'd flick on and off all the switches. She'd show them Sammy's bunk bed with the red metal frames, a childhood bed, going on the Yard Sale list, for sure. He only used the top bunk, anyway, the bottom bunk was filled with orange traffic cones, she had no idea why. Also a number of orange vinyl flags. She'd been meaning to ask. She'd point out Sammy's inflatable John Kerry punching bag to the touring parent, saying "Dirk gave him that." Kerry would be drooping to one side, having been kicked as well as punched. A bit of sand leaking from the base. "He's so messy!" she'd shriek, meaning Sammy, not John.

~

8.

She had worked for a bit on the Nader campaign, back when, pressed into service by her neighbor Sara Greeley-Greenough, who was active with WIM (Women in Mourning), protesting this 'n that. But she only did it, stuffed the envelopes and whatnot, to get Dirk's goat, and also so she could add it to her resume. She couldn't get into the WIM thing, the standing on the bridge in widow's weeds, carrying signs that said War Is Obsolete. Clearly, it wasn't. Plus it was hard to work WIM into your schedule, and standing stock-still gained no aerobic benefit, and the widow thing made Dirk nervous. Getting his goat was sufficient.

She liked to add something to her resume every few years. She would get it out and read it. Then she would get in the Suburban and drive to Target with her list. Orange-scented Swipes. Another plastic hamper. Bounce, Bon Ami, Febreze. Sammy's snack crackers and power drinks. Secretly, she had liked Gore. Al Gore, with the smooth hair and implacable smile. A hint of latent muscularity. Once she and Ellen, her neighbor across the street, had posed in front of a cardboard stand-up poster of Al Gore, taking pictures with their cell phones. Where had that been? The mall. They'd been doing the Shop-for-a-Cause. Five percent of the day's purchases going to breast cancer. The photos of Ellen showed her dressed from tip to toe in Breast Cancer Awareness pink, even her earrings. She was holding high her Virgin Mary and laughing. They were taking a break at Surfer Joe's, celebrating their new, matching haircuts. (Non-alcoholic for Ellen, alcohol being a risk factor.) There were life-sized cardboard actors and music stars at Surfer Joe's—Kevin Bacon, Michael Jackson, Elvis. But no other candidates were there, cardboard or otherwise. Only Al.

Later she dreamt about Al. In her dream he said, "You have an unusual sense of color." It was a compliment. He also said, "I like your full-on Twiggy pixie cut," but she knew upon waking that those weren't his words at all, they were the words of her stylist, Mari. In the dream the words had flooded her with warmth, a feeling of being really, finally, unprecedentedly, understood. But upon waking she felt a bit foolish and somehow betrayed.

~

9.

She went ahead and voted for Nader. Sara Greeley-Greenough watched her do it at the kitchen counter bar, the early voting ballot. Sara made her get it, and then she monitored the voting almost at knifepoint. Well, steak knife. At a barbeque, a Neighborhood Association thing, their turn. Sara made both her and Ellen complete the request form for absentee ballots for the early voting, then she hounded them daily until the ballots were completed and sent, the deed done. Fat lot of good.

Ellen voted for Gore (which Sara said she respected, as if she'd been asked), and she voted for Nader, to get Dirk's goat, but she really didn't mind all *that* much Dirk's man Bush, Bush the Younger, "W," and at first she found him sort of sexy, too, though there was no one she could tell that to. His jeans and all. Working on the ranch. His full head of hair. (She for sure couldn't say that to Ellen, who by then was doing chemo.) A certain cuteness about the mouth, a little boy quality. And then his small animal look when he addressed the nation about the twin towers. Scared. He addressed the nation looking slightly upward toward the camera, as if he were peering out of a hole. He was scared, "skeered," as he might say. It made her want to mother him or big sister him, or something.

But then there was Afghanistan, and then there was Iraq, and then Ellen's son Alex went off to boot camp, right out of high school, lured by the promises of the recruiters out at the mall. Ellen and her second husband, Coach Murphy, had been super surprised, since there was a little college money, at least to start out. Ellen thought Alex had a good chance at a music scholarship. Coach said if he'd stuck with the soccer, even better, but he didn't, so ok then.

Dwayne had encouraged him, turns out. Dwayne was Alex's father, Ellen's first husband, the guy she was married to the first time she got cancer. After Ellen got cancer, when Alex was thirteen, she said she was rearranging her priorities and Dwayne didn't even make the list. She left Dwayne and married Coach, whom she met through his sister Celeste, her divorce lawyer, who had a side business as a life coach. (Celeste said you have to be married to *someone*!) Immediately after chemo Ellen got pregnant with little Alexis, which Celeste encouraged, as it was life-giving. No more chemo centers, just birthing units. Celeste said she was thrilled, thrilled, that Ellen was having a girl, and Ellen said she was thrilled too, she was tired of boys. Just in general, she said to Alex. Not you.

Dwayne pointed out to Alex the job skills and also the travel opportunities. As did the military representatives at Career Day at the high school. As did the recruiters out at the mall, the buff looking boys at the tables.

Gone off on the train, like in a movie. Only 17 when he enlisted, Dwayne signed the papers. Off on the train to boot camp in California. Alex said that after boot camp he'd probably be stationed in Hawaii.

~

10.

Second time around, Ellen had a double mastectomy. Flat as a pancake! No surgical strike, this was a full-on attack. More chemo, fine, bring it on. Chemical warfare. She said it with a high, shrill laugh, her eyes full of tears.

She was trying hard to be very positive in her attitude because Celeste told her that being upbeat would beat it. Moping was harmful. You made yourself sick that way. Well, sicker. It was all about lifestyle. Probably she had made herself sick in the first place with a poor lifestyle and negative thinking. Or it might have been due to Dwayne. She should have left Dwayne earlier. She was too passive.

Celeste herself was a breast cancer survivor and for her it had become a whole second career. She organized events and parades and blogged about awareness and finding a cure. Her blogs focused on tales of heroines, the mother of four who had a double mastectomy then went on to run a marathon, or the smart entrepreneur who designed a better wig, easy to wear and cool in the summer. For Celeste, these were the heroines of illness, vanquishers wielding invisible swords. The enemies were poor lifestyles and bad attitudes. No victims here! She injected a determined humor into her postings about treatment ("Slash and Burn") and surgical reconstruction ("Unit A and Unit B"). She called her humor "Vitamin H." Vitamin

H was essential to the upbeat energy needed to beat it. Her humor was aggressive and relentless, on the alert for Ellen's deficiencies.

"Beat it! . . . Beat it!" Alex sang the Michael Jackson song to show his awareness of breast cancer (a hard thing for men to say, never mind boys, especially "breast"). A Celeste idea, she filmed Alex, who was embarrassed but willing, and she gave the DVD to Ellen as a surprise present right before her surgery. Later, it was incorporated into the slideshow at Alex's Celebration of Life, part of the visual tribute. Half the town watched Alex sing the song and do the dance moves, or try to, jerking his body across the slick tile in the family kitchen, pulling his hands in to his stomach, a sudden spasm, hunching over, spinning around like he'd been shot.

~

II.

Alex used to babysit Sammy, he used to play freeze tag with Sammy and his friends for hours in the front yard, and when they were past the toddler age but still preteen, he would take them trick-or-treating. Sammy and his little friends called Alex their "Big." Big brother, big boss, who knew? They loved their Big. They would go over and ring Alex's doorbell and say "Can our Big chase us?" And he did, even after he got to high school.

Alex used to do a lot of things. He used to come to the door selling band candy, right up through senior year, trying to keep his face blank and impassive, and then it just flowed into the sweetest smile, and he'd say "How's it going?" Always fundraising in the neighborhood for school things. A faint shadow of down on his upper lip, if he moved his head a certain way. Still getting his growth. He was good, he'd say, things were going good. Probably he'd be stationed in Hawaii. He showed her the brochure he kept in his backpack, a recruitment flyer from the Navy, a guy hang gliding off a rock-faced cliff toward a long, sandy beach.

Ever hear that little voice that says Get a Life? The brochure said. *It just got louder.*

Gone off and killed the first month. A car bomb, those IED whatevers, roadside explosion. Alex and his unit had been on their way to rout out the insurgents. Operation Shock Wave Whatever.

After that, she didn't want to vote for anyone at all, which, from the perspective of Alex, she knew, didn't really matter.

She would just hold it together. Forget voting. Forget about the protesting this 'n thats. She would stick to her classes, her wellness and her fitness. She would get in the Suburban and drive to Target with her list, doing Kegel exercises at the stoplights to keep her uterus from falling out. Tend to one's self. Support the family. Orange-scented Swipes, Bon Ami, Febreze, natural air fresheners, aromatic oils with bamboo diffusers. Boxers for little Sammy. A teenager now, but still. *Little.* Men's xxx-small.

~

The insurgents did it. Dirk said they were mercenaries, a word which somehow made her think of shopping baskets, the square plastic kind at Albertson's that you hang on your arm. Dirk said, "There's no room for discourse!" and this for some reason made her think of arugula, which she was getting into.

Lately, whenever Bush approached a microphone on TV his lips moved a tiny bit before any sound came out, like he was talking to himself. Now that was creepy.

~

12.

She couldn't tell if Dirk liked her full-on Twiggy pixie cut. He didn't say. He said, "You cut your hair." He refused to commit an opinion. He was like Bush, who said, "We are working to defeat the terrorists, the killers," when someone asked him about Hurricane Katrina.

"Remember how radical Twiggy seemed?" She said this to Mari, then remembered that Mari was probably thirty-plus years younger than she. She couldn't really talk to Mari about much beyond styling gels. She wondered where Mari got her Twiggy knowledge, probably from something on TV. Mari had probably been fifteen years away from being born when Twiggy had disconcerted the world with her unabashedly boyish body and full-on pixie cut. Twiggy and go-go boots and bra burning and flag burning. She herself had only been fourteen or so when all that was going on. She remembered her father recoiling in his recliner, looking at photos of Twiggy in *Time*. He said she looked like a war refugee. He recoiled the same way when *Life* magazine published the picture of the skinny little Vietnamese girl being napalmed. He was affronted by Twiggy and by the skinny little Vietnamese girl with no clothes on. The napalm he didn't mention.

Her father was repelled by the monk in the robe, burning like liquid on the pavement. Self-immolation. On a busy intersection.

In the middle of the day. Seated on the pavement in the lotus position. It was on TV. This was not like standing on a street corner,
some non-aerobic exercise of protest. This was not a reenactment
on the History Channel, such as you might see now, men running
to and fro, planes flying in formation. There was no background
music, for one thing. There were no logos on the screen identifying
the associated conflict, no sports scores or weather updates scroll-
ing across beneath. There was just a burst of flame, then flickering diminishment, the monk's body a still statue, carved, upright,
then suddenly slumped sideways, reduced, his face and shaven skull
sharply delineated within the fire.

Her father said he didn't think they should show these kinds of
things on TV. Then he just watched.

~

13.

She and Ellen had been Sunnyside Moms together, back when Ellen was married to Dwayne. They hadn't overlapped much in the activities, though, since Alex had been a kindergartner, an older Minnow, when Sammy was in the preschool, barely a hatchling Shark. Later they became workout partners mostly, taking turns driving, covering each other on the excuses to the WIM women, that sort of thing. They'd never been super close, not really. Ellen had tried to get her involved in the Be Beautiful business, which was Ellen's occupation outside the home. She sold Be Beautiful products at house parties; there were pink martinis and it was fun. And then, after her diagnosis, Ellen became involved in Be Beautiful Cosmetics for the Cure and Kiss Breast Cancer Good-Bye cause-marketing campaigns. Half the proceeds of certain products went to the Be Beautiful Foundation's programs for breast cancer. Ellen sort of stumbled over giving the explanations, not being real comfortable in an advocacy role. Usually she just gave you the flyer. Glowing women with long hair, heads thrown back in laughter.

Celeste applauded these efforts, saying Ellen was really coming into her own, getting out of her comfort zone, not easy. You go, girl! But Sara Greeley-Greenough said the products Be Beautiful sold for its campaign were laden with carcinogenic chemicals. Those pink-tubed lipsticks named Crusade Rose, Determined Red,

Cherub Cheer, Courageous Coral? Lethal as hell. She cited articles, dropped off clippings.

Really, when it came down to it, her bond with her neighbor Ellen mostly was forged through their shared annoyance at Celeste's patronizing cheerleading and their mutual agreement that Sara was one major downer. But no, they themselves weren't really all that close. Girlfriends, they called each other that.

~

14.

Two men in uniform, hats in hand. Alex's little half-sister Alexis opened the door to them. Alex's dog Cartman, a Springer Spaniel with mental problems, barked madly and nipped at one of the men's stiff, starched pant leg. Ellen said they looked like soldiers from *Babes in Toyland,* which she'd helped paint sets for in junior high. A light opera. Their cheeks were very smooth and pink, as if they'd been dusted with foundation makeup, tinted a little. She reflected on this later. At the moment of the encounter, she just stood there with a DustBuster in her hand. (Chemo, she'd claim, made her want to clean.) She kept saying, What? What? As if she were hard of hearing. *Wha? Wha?* Alex's little half-sister Alexis echoed her mother. *Wha??* She was only three.

"We regret to inform you." Like in a movie. Ellen repeated it later, incredulous, hardly able yet to cry, or even breathe, and her little daughter Alexis repeated it herself several times more.

We wegwet, we wegwet . . .

~

Sammy's reaction had been weird when they all talked about it as a family at The Family Meal. Dirk went into a harangue about all the increasingly intractable problems, except he called them "untrackable." He talked about unacceptable conditions and the commitment to finding a solution. He said "impact" and "consensus" and lots of other words. The Iraqis needed to step up to the plate. They needed to take charge, quit being victims. The problem was their mentality. They did not have the right attitude. It was in their culture.

A little smile played around Sammy's lips while his eyes filled with tears. She understood. She understood he probably was thinking: *This is happening and I can see myself in it, but I'm also looking back at myself being part of this story and how I act and all.*

He didn't say much out loud. He just said, "Dead?"

~

15.

After Alex left on the train, Ellen started opting out. She put it positively like that. She wasn't stopping, she was starting. Starting to opt out. She said she was setting her priorities. Well ok. They'd wave at each other, getting their mail. And then the news came, the uniforms at the door. And, after a few days, Ellen just stopped. She sat in her living room, motionless. Celeste had to do all the planning for Alex's Celebration of Life, the big party that followed the service and burial. She had to get the slideshow of Alex's life organized, hire the hall, arrange for parking, get the balloons, have caterers prepare boxes and boxes of MacAttack Mac 'n Cheese, Alex's favorite food when he was ten. She did it for Ellen, she said, she did it for Alex, she did it as a gift to the city. She was interviewed by the paper. She got the entire high school jazz band involved.

Then everyone went home. Celeste told Ellen to take her Vitamin H and stay active and engaged. Grief, she said, was a process. Ellen said she felt like the last leaf on the tree, about to fall. And then she spiraled down.

When Ellen died there was no Celebration of Life. Her parents had a private service right there at the crematorium, in the chapel of the mausoleum, the name for the climate-controlled storage hall for loved one's cremains. But the Celebration was postponed. Celeste said they were planning it for the following summer, to coincide with vacations. (She and Murph were still settling bills from the Celebration for Alex!) She said there were a lot of different schedules to work around before they could even send out a Save the Date.

~

One day Murph came across the street with all of Ellen's pink-wear, the baseball caps, the workout clothes, even the earrings. Also a shoebox full of unsold Be Beautiful products, the Be Beautiful Kiss Breast Cancer Good-Bye Brilliant Moisture Lipcolor in the thin, pink tubes. He didn't ask her if she wanted this, he just mutely handed it over.

She didn't wear or use any of it. In fact, she took it all to Secret Treasure right away, feeling guilty, but still. Her drawers and closets were stuffed.

~

16.

When Sammy was one, then two, then three years old, he and she used to take naps together. They would lie entwined in each other's arms listening to the Owl Moon tape.

... there was no wind ... the trees stood still as giant statues ... and the moon was so bright the sky seemed to shine ...

When it got to the part about the train, the sound of its whistle gliding across the snowy fields through the dark night ... *long and low, like a sad, sad song* ... they both would be very sleepy. Sometimes Sammy would stroke her cheek with one hand while they listened, and she would think *This is happening and I see us lying on the bed together, I feel Sammy's hand on my cheek, and I will think of this, I will remember this, years from now when Sammy is a teenager and in danger ... driving cars ... in danger ... having sex and drinking beer ... smoking pot ...*

And then she went to sleep.

~

17.

The postal service issued a decree that mail carriers count their steps. The average stride was somehow determined and the exact distance of each route was measured and the mail carriers were required to submit their steps. Total them up. This was to find out if they dilly-dallied. If she was raking leaves around the noon hour, planning the rest of her day, she might engage the mail carrier, a stern young man, in conversation. But he had to answer on the fly. He didn't seem prone to conversation anyway, mostly offering just a curt nod of his head to her comments about the leaves and the weather and the forecast and her apologies for Sammy's skate ramps all over the yard.

Sometimes he handed the mail directly to her, and this was a bit embarrassing for both of them, a quick intimacy. If this happened she did not attempt any conversation beyond "Thanks." He, in turn, might say "Afternoon," a verification. That was it for talking. He'd hand off the mail and they both would be careful that no fingers touched. Bills. Pizza flyers. More AARP stuff, addressed to her, not Dirk, who shuddered if he even saw it.

Globe and Cosmos, in its brown paper wrapper.

"Here's your porn." Sammy would say, picking up *Globe and Cosmos* from the dining room table. He recently had been trying out words like that. Porn, douchebag, pimp, Jesus H. Christ. H? *What's the H for?* she'd ask. He didn't know, whatever. Except he'd say, "What-ev-ah!"

and flap his wrist, pretending he was gay. He wasn't old enough hardly to be anything, in her mind, and here he was pretending to be the other thing. He'd stand there at the refrigerator in just his boxers at two in the afternoon on a Saturday, squaring his thin shoulders and flexing his baby bird chest, his fragile bones exposed, his collarbones, his pelvic bones, his skinny legs and long, delicate toes.

Porn. This had all started with public school. Parts. That's what the teachers at Butler School said was covered in Sex Ed. They said this at the parent-teacher conference. "Just parts." At Sunnyside, Sammy's progressive Early Childhood learning center, where he went until third grade ("Pre Through Three"), there had been contextualized instruction. There was "Good Touch, Bad Touch," a special unit taught by Sara Greeley-Greenough as a parent volunteer. How to avoid child molesters. Useful information, if somewhat improvised. ("If I were to offer you candy . . . If I were to touch you here.") The little Minnows sat transfixed. The 1st-3rd combo class had taken a vote and settled on Minnows for their name. They liked to think of themselves as fish, just silver streaks of intelligence and joy.

Sara held up a pointer to a poster of the human body, which was not only stripped bare of clothing, but completely skinless, being an anatomical chart, a complicated map of muscles and bones. Her pointer hovered in the groin area. "Don't touch!" the Minnows chorused, bursting into gleeful laughter.

Porn. She couldn't say why *Globe and Cosmos* arrived all covered up that way in brown paper. Unwrapping it, she found a black man on the front, peering out from gauzy headgear. Not a porn star, of course, and not a tribal anyone, either, as one might have thought upon first glance. No, the black man turned out to be a HazMat worker, wearing plastic.

The Toxins in the Closet, said the cover. *What You Can't See Can Kill You.*

~

18.

If Al had won back then . . . well, no one would ever know. In their super-Republican state it hadn't really mattered, a vote for Nader, a vote for Gore, it hadn't mattered. Not one whit. The Supreme Court decided, anyway.

Dirk went into his harangues at dinnertime, using words from city council meetings.

"A solicitation has been issued inviting communities to propose the implementation . . ." She had no idea what he was talking about, other than the fact that Our Troops in Iraq as a topic somehow had flowed into the Municipal Youth Drug Court. She pictured tattooed youths wearing robes and powdered wigs. Then Dirk was back on Our Troops, comparing them favorably to local miscreants, fine, young citizens vs. deadbeat stoners, and she saw Alex in the official 8x10 photograph displayed at his funeral service, his face small and worried under the big hat.

"The city is committed to integrating the Reclaiming Futures model with best practices." When Dirk was on a roll like this Sammy would give her his "What the fuck?" look—if he looked at either of them at all. If Dirk realized he was being ignored, he might say, "This really gets my dandruff up!" an inside joke for the three of them, something Dirk used to say for real until the umpteenth correction finally purged it from his vocabulary. But they were in bad moods these days, she and Sammy, and weren't likely to respond to inside jokes, so all Dirk could do was violently clear his throat as he stacked the dishes, until he finally had to go to the bathroom to hack up some phlegm. Then he went in and turned on the TV.

Dirk went to city council meetings the way some men watched Monday night football. She didn't quite get it. He never provided public input and on some occasions seemed only vaguely aware of what was on the agenda. Briefly, she thought that maybe he was doing something else, not going to city council meetings at all. Maybe he was engaged in a covert activity. So one Monday night she turned on Channel 13, the community channel that chose to air those meetings in their mind-numbing entirety, pretending even to herself that she was just surfing. There he was, in the front row, rapt.

~

She thought she detected a strange smell in the house. Not a bad smell, just different. A hint of something familiar, flowery, yet . . . strange. Introduced from without. She sniffed Clark, thinking Dirk or Sammy might have shampooed him, although that was unlikely. Usually they all just sprayed him with Febreze. This wasn't that. She asked Dirk and Sammy, "What's that smell?"

"What smell?" Dirk answered.

"What smell?" said Sammy.

"I don't smell any smell," they both said. "What's it smell like?"

So many of their conversations seemed to go like this.

"I don't know," she said. "Just different."

~

III.

THE LEAVES

19.

Her laundry day was Monday, in the morning. There was a ripped and faded printout about it down in the laundry room. #1A—Monday a.m. She set her alarm Sunday night for six a.m. so she could get down there early and not overlap too much with #1B, who was also on Monday mornings.

For a good long while, #1B had been a tiny old man, fragile as a leaf. Talking was something neither of them had desired, but she had looked forward to their brief encounter at the end of her laundry time. He had worn faded flannel shirts with the long sleeves buttoned down. Underneath the plaid could be glimpsed several more layers, a turtleneck under a worn thermal t-shirt, no matter the season or the weather. His limp khaki pants were held up with suspenders, long underwear appearing at the hems when he slowly bent down to pick up a dropped sock. The cuffs of the long underwear were tucked neatly into his tightly laced logger boots.

The old man had been a kindred soul. As he entered the laundry room on Monday mornings at 8:00 a.m., carrying his small plastic basket with one pair of pants and one faded shirt and one tattered turtleneck carefully concealing the layer beneath, the layer that was his underwear and socks, she might just be leaving with her somewhat larger plastic basket carrying one bath towel, one hand towel, one wash cloth, one blouse and one pair of slacks, her socks and underwear and nightgown hidden beneath. And they might smile and nod at each other, the little old man's lips suddenly cracking wide.

She had many clothes, purchased at the Bargain Box and Secret Treasure, her closet and drawers were stuffed. She even had some in boxes under her bed and on the built-in shelves in the dark hallway and in the tiny bathroom. But under her various coats and jackets, hats and umbrellas, she only wore these, the blouse and the slacks, or another similar set. Upstairs, the same worn cardigan sweater that she wore day in and day out hung on the kitchen chair back. She collected things but only really varied the hats, the wide-brimmed hats and the baseball caps and the woolen berets, as well as a more modest collection of coats: long woolen coats, rain coats, ski jackets with zippers. Her baseball caps might have writing. Ole's Service Center. The Nature Conservancy. NRA. United States Air Force. Sunnyside School. Some days she wore a denim jean jacket and a baseball cap and imagined she was her little brother Eddy.

Her other secret treasures, her inner layers, were mostly just to have. For collecting, not for wearing. She liked to organize them and look at them, then hide them back away. They made her feel fortified, equipped, prepared. They gave her pleasure, in and of themselves, a spiritual luxury. They filled up her heart, momentarily.

She laundered the yellow comforter once a month, along with her sheets, devoting her wash time just to that. She set her alarm for 5:30 a.m. on those particular Mondays, to allow for plenty of time. She didn't know what the little old man used for sheets or towels or wash cloths, and she sometimes wondered.

~

Every day, no matter the weather, the old man would emerge from #1B at ten a.m. bundled into a greasy green jacket and wearing large cotton gardening gloves and a lumpy gray cap with a visor and ear flaps. Slowly, he would descend the four front steps and fish out the rake hidden beneath them. Then he methodically raked the patch of lawn in front of the building, starting at the brick walls and working out to the street in rows. He did this every season of the year. She sat at her kitchen table, drank her morning tea, and heard the scraping swish of the rake. In the summer he raked the lawn, accumulating a small pile of dead grass and twigs. In the fall he raked leaves into big piles at the curb. In the winter he raked the snow, and if there was a heavy snowfall he raked the top of the snow. He did this from ten to eleven a.m., and then he disappeared back inside #1B, not to be seen again that day.

Food for the old man was delivered by taxi, two plastic bags, every Friday. Several cans of fruit cocktail, a quart of milk, a loaf of Wonder Bread, a package of bologna, a package of Kraft cheese, a half-carton of eggs and one individual-sized box of animal crackers. Sometimes a single roll of toilet paper in crinkly white wrapping. She had occasion to peek inside the bags out in the foyer as she passed in or out, edging past the taxi driver, who carried the bags to the door of #1B. On every such occasion the contents appeared to be more or less the same.

The taxi driver's name, *Dave*, was embroidered in curlicue letters on his jacket, and he wore large black-framed glasses held together on one side with a paperclip. Dave left a few flyers from Albertson's in the foyer with information about the store's own delivery service. But the little old man preferred to give his unvarying list straight to Dave. Each Friday they had a hand off. The groceries were delivered and Dave walked away with the next week's list, which must have been identical, or nearly, to the list he'd just fulfilled.

~

The new tenant of #1B was a noisy boy who wore a rumpled top-coat and long chains dangling from his pants. His head was shaved bald, which made his ears look large. He had a frightening zigzag down the back of his head, as if his scalp had been split open and then sewn shut. Sometimes he wore an old-fashioned black bowler hat, which puzzled her. Sometimes he smoked cigars, the thick, sweet smell lingering in the hallway long after he'd gone out, making her queasy. She could hear him clumping and jangling as he came and went, slamming the door.

The little old man's comings and goings had been soft as a whisper. The rake's scrape had been like the scratching of a mouse. But it didn't take her more than half of one morning to realize that the sound had ended and he was gone.

~

20.

She could hear him in there, #1B, she could hear him on the phone. First she would hear him pacing, then she would hear him talking, saying "What the fuck!" and "No way!" and "That sonuvabitch, that Son. Of. A. Bitch!"

"Jesus H. Christ!!" he would exclaim at nearly a shout, and then she would hear a thump, as if he'd smacked something.

This usually began after ten o'clock at night. The tiny old man would have been asleep by then, and normally so would she, or nearly. Normally, she would be lying there under the yellow comforter, waiting for the train that announced its arrival at 10:20, signaling to the citizens a cautionary note, only gently disrupting the peace in its primal way, the long, drawn-out call a mournful question.

But nothing was normal now. Not since the arrival of this noisy boy in #1B.

She could hear him in there, pacing. Talking on the phone. She didn't have a phone. She once had thought a phone might be required, so had looked in the yellow pages under Telephones, but then she had given up. She wished the young man with the jangling chains had given up.

"Jesus fucking Christ!!" She could hear him talking on the phone. He never seemed happy with the conversation. She could hear him pacing and then . . . *thump* . . . she heard him hit something, the wall maybe, or the door.

Normally, she might call the landlord. She knew that normally that is something one might do. But, truth be told, she didn't know the landlord. She didn't know who the landlord was, didn't know his name. She put money in an envelope marked Garden Gate Rentals and pushed it through a slot at the Garden Gate office, near the post office, and that was that for landlords. She missed the presence of the old man, his visible Monday morning presence and his invisible presence behind his door. She missed his daily sojourns out to rake the world, tidying and tending. She missed the weekly visits of the cab driver Dave, with his toothy smile and black, crooked eyeglasses.

But she didn't deviate from her pattern. Her heart was full of missing, but her pattern remained. She counted the bills out carefully and put them in an envelope and licked the envelope and labeled it "#1A" and put it in her satchel. Then she shoved it through the slot beside the Garden Gate office door on her way to First Wednesday.

She had no idea when this had started and no idea how it might end.

~

21.

There were three possible waitresses on Wednesday and this particular waitress was her favorite. She had glossy bangs and a low, liquid voice. She spoke little and her tone was quiet, but it was easy to imagine her singing.

She did not say, "Well how are we today?" as if she were a nurse. She did not say. "Here ya go!" when bringing the bread, as if she were a volunteer at Christmas time bringing a toy. She did not say, "Oh-*kay*," when she took the order in the first place, as if the ordering and delivery of soup and salad were an exciting adventure, an arduous task finally agreed upon, a great collaboration. She simply raised her eyebrows, with no indication of any memory of any other Wednesday, and said, "Ready to order?" in her calm, quiet voice and nodded in a serious way as she wrote.

She had beautiful hands. The fingers were long and thin and pale with blue veins. She wore no rings. Her nails were trimmed closely and polished with a clear shine. She had a writer's bump on the third finger of her right hand, the hand that held the pen for taking orders. She had hair to her chin, thick and chestnut brown. Occasionally she flicked at her hair with her writing hand, the pen barely missing her eyes, which were large, clear, and violet.

"Tell Audrey," she heard the cook say to the cashier on a frosty October Wednesday, a day well suited to wearing one of the cold season woolen berets and pleasurable for walking. She had brought a satchel with acrylic gloves inside, in case the sun didn't quite burn off the chill. But she wanted to keep the gloves off for now, thinking to sample the hand lotion at Macy's.

"Audrey!" the cashier called across the room and this waitress looked up from her pad, her eyebrows raised to indicate she had heard. "No more pasta."

She herself already had her pasta salad, maybe the last of the lot. She was nearly finished with it, in fact, bite number nine. It tasted very good.

Audrey. Something about that name. A name from childhood. Audrey the Good Little Witch. Smooth hair, a magic wand. Smiling, shadowless, normal. Always a happy ending. Audrey. *Audrey awloo*. That's what Eddy would say.

~

22.

The leaf blower's painful whine drowned out all other sound. She could see the tree branches moving, but could hear no wind, nothing but the whine. The sound of the receding bus also was obliterated by the leaf blower, which was dispelling leaves and tranquility at an even pace. This Wednesday had become a bus day because there was construction outside of Macy's and her usual entrance was closed. She had hesitated at the boardwalk detour, the flimsy, narrow walkway. Then she had turned back.

The man wielding the leaf blower wore protective headphones. He was a tall man in a sweat suit, his carriage both lanky and stiff. She walked up the street purposefully, noting the styrofoam tombstones that had sprouted on the lawns like mushrooms since her last visit.

Here lies Hugh. He thought he had the flu.

Hugh, flu, Hugh, flu. It wasn't quite a rhyme. That bothered her.

She already had her Halloween candy. She planned to put it in the blue plastic bowl on Halloween night and then turn out the light, the hallway light that hung over her door, the door for #1A. She always turned out that light on Halloween night to discourage trick-or-treaters. She also turned out the rose lamp, inside. When she turned out the rose lamp she had no light at all. She couldn't practice her words. But she didn't want to go to bed before her bedtime, so she just sat there in the rocker and rocked quietly, trying not to make a sound. Occasionally she might hear a noise from the street, kids shouting, somebody laughing. These were older kids, college kids maybe, since the downtown bars were only a few blocks away. Usually she heard nothing inside the building, no one out in the hallway on Halloween night. But she couldn't predict what might happen this year, with the new presence of #1B.

Every year she filled the blue plastic bowl with cellophane bags of candy corn, tiny boxes of Chiclets, and jewel-colored suckers, the handles soft loops. Then she turned out the lights, the hall light and the rose lamp. She sat in the rocker and listened.

On November 1, All Souls' Day, she carefully emptied the contents of the bowl back into the plastic grocery sack and stowed it away in its designated spot on the top right hand shelf of the closet, about midway down.

~

She noticed that her house on the quiet Butler Creek block also had Halloween decorations. Many small ghosts hung from the weeping birch tree, twirling in the breeze. They were made from little squares of white cloth, pieces of a sheet perhaps, that somebody had cut up and rubber-banded around small balls, lightweight and floating, maybe ping-pong balls. The ball heads all were suspended from the tree by threads around their necks.

An artificial jack-o-lantern grinned next to the brass dachshund. She rang the doorbell and listened for the delayed chime. She knew that the real dog was on the other side of the door, perversely quiet. She rang the doorbell again and waited, willing herself not to turn around to look at the man with the leaf blower. Its noise continued, a steady drill of sound.

She would say, "Is there a bus that serves this neighborhood?" Her heart pounded, hard, as always, not at the thought of any deception, but at the thought of talking like that, beginning an exchange, and also at the thought of soon entering. She closed her eyes and counted very slowly to five. *One aw-loo, two aw-loo . . .*

When she opened the door and stepped inside the dog clicked backwards a few steps, almost respectfully, alert, part challenge, part deference. He sloped onto his rump and watched her. He barked once, an afterthought. Then he was quiet. He knew the routine and followed her with his eyes as she entered the quiet glade of the living room and eased into the high-backed chair, with its dogs and horses and frozen men in red. He held this position for the usual few minutes and then clicked away, off into the kitchen where she suspected he kept his toys. When she left he might appear with one in his mouth, monitoring her departure.

The tree outside was almost stripped bare. It was breezier up here than in the center of town. The room was the same except this day it needed dusting. She could see a thin film all across the coffee table. There was a new *Globe and Cosmos. The Secrets of Living Longer.* On the front cover, a man stood on his head, his legs brown and his belly showing.

She opened her satchel and took out her acrylic gloves. She put them on and stood up and leaned over the coffee table and ran her hands all over it, in and among the magazines and the silver packet of matches in their little crystal saucer next to the pale, fat candle. She sat and looked at the table, leaning over to dab at a spot she had missed. Across the street the leaf blower whined on and on, constant and annoying. This was not like the old man's rake, the scritch-scratch rustling sound of the old man's gentle tending of the earth. This was just an attack, mindless, arbitrary, efficient.

Leaves, yes or no.

~

23.

Halloween. They waited for the train. If you didn't move, if you stared straight ahead, the gap between the train cars became visible, a stop-start movie, a flickering view of the other side, the street corner with a yellow fire hydrant, the street light, the beauty parlor just beyond, the OPEN sign glowing red in the window until six o'clock and sometimes, forgotten, all night.

The best part had been ringing the doorbell of just any house and having it open almost instantly, the greeter feigning surprise. She and Eddy would peek inside, seeing a bit, catching a glimpse of a bald-headed man watching TV, or a family still at dinner, their heads turned, some of them smiling. She would save the images for later, the knickknacks on top of the piano, the family photos, the doily-covered armchairs, the dried flower arrangements in baskets on little tables, the TVs on TV stands, the magazine racks, the ency-clopedias, the lamps, the books, the coats on coat hooks, the warm, steamy, cooking smells, the dry furnace smells, the dogs wagging their tails or raising their heads or barking shrilly, the cats blink-ing from their perches. All this in a glimpse, which then became a preoccupation, a musing dream.

Eddy wore his cracked, hard-plastic Casper the Ghost mask. That was it, no white sheet or Kmart ghost costume, just his regular pants and jacket. She might wear a large kerchief and one earring, a gypsy lady. Or she patted her face with dirt and wore a battered hat, a hobo. Once she found a black feather on the sidewalk, a neat, shiny arc. She stuck it in a green baseball cap and called herself Peter Pan. Another year she made a witch's hat from black poster paper, a flat base, a spiraled cone. Audrey the Good Little Witch, a pencil as a wand. You could be anyone at Halloween and people smiled.

Eddy was after the candy, and afterwards he would lay his haul out on the floor in neat rows, Hershey's aligned with Hershey's, Life Savers with Life Savers, bubble gum with bubble gum. He would make "campfires" with the Pixy Stix, balanced tripods, all in a row. He would stack the Tootsie Rolls like cordwood and make little brick houses from the Bit-O-Honey's, the round Necco's providing cobblestone walks.

But for her it was the crossing over, or nearly, the tingling edge that felt so exhilarating, scary and heady, like stepping your toe over the line in a game of sticks, a quick jab into foreignness, a poke at forbidden territory, an opening up, the loose, lovely feeling of a foyer.

Out on the streets dry leaves clattered into drifts, the clouds crossed the sky like slow ships, the moon moved off the mountain, and sometimes she and Eddy went back out, doggedly working the walks, their breath moist, Eddy wheezing behind his mask. They rang doorbells until all the houses went dark and no one answered.

~

24.

The man with the leaf blower was finished. Silence rushed in to fill the corners. She leaned forward in her chair to get a view of him through the window. He had his back to her and was watching his garage door open in response to the gadget he held in his hand. He extended his hand toward the door, holding his arm out as if giving an order or blessing. An American flag flapped next to the front door of the man's long, low, brick house. The door was flanked by drooping corn husks tied in bundles and a smaller, faded "Harvest Festival" flag decorated with pumpkins hung above the doorbell.

He disappeared into the garage with his leaf blower and protective headphones, squeezing his oversized body between two SUVs, identical except for color, one apple red, one forest green. The cars were shiny and clean, as was the garage. Yellow ribbon "Support Our Troops" decals were positioned in the same spot on the right rear window of each car, with pink ribbon Breast Cancer Awareness decals on the left. She could glimpse shelves with tools and lawn equipment and hoses, neatly curled. She remembered seeing this man a week earlier hosing off his driveway, methodically aiming the arc at invisible pebbles or twigs.

He came back out of the garage now and turned to watch the door descend. Then he surveyed the effects of his leaf blowing. A few leaves from her weeping birch tree had already drifted over onto his driveway. He leaned over and picked them up and put them in his pocket. Then he stood staring at her house, rocking back on the heels of his big white gym shoes. He performed a stretch, his hands behind his head, a brief seesaw, side to side, keeping his gaze on the relatively haphazard lawn across the street, with its lumber and such, her lawn, the lawn of her house. She knew that the lumber was for skateboarding, that skateboarders hauled this wreckage out into the street and then leapt at it, their boards magically clinging to their feet as they executed slides and jumps and tricks punctuated with a rough clatter. She noticed this on her walks, so she knew what she was looking at now, out there on the lawn. On her walks she always cringed at the noise of the skateboarders, although she always turned to look.

The clock on the mantel made its grinding sound and chimed the half hour. She rose and walked three steps to the built-in bookcase. She opened her satchel and peered in. It was empty, except for her bus transfer, tucked into a side pocket, and a smaller zipped bag, with *Estee Lauder* stitched on the side in apricot-colored thread against a bright plaid. BEAUTY appeared beneath it, in block letters stamped in gold.

She still had on her acrylic gloves. Scanning the bookshelves, she found an opening between a thick book, *It*, by Stephen King, and a slimmer book with the long title of *French Women Don't Get Fat*. She gently tucked the BEAUTY bag between the books, pushing it with her finger until it was almost out of sight.

~

25.

Another day, another Wednesday. The construction at Macy's was completed, the sidewalk free. She had her lunch, chewing the macaroni slowly, counting, and then she set off to use the free samples of lotion and perfume. She avoided the eyes of the counter lady as she squirted and sprayed. And then she pulled on her acrylic gloves and continued on her way. Today she was Eddy, in her denim jean jacket and baseball cap. The cap said *Vulcan!* and had a picture of a skateboard with wings. Baseball caps were 50 cents at Secret Treasure. There were many of them, piled up in a bin.

This time she turned left off the river walking path and headed up California Street to the Bargain Box. She preferred Secret Treasure, in terms of the selection, but felt that she was watched by the women there, just as she was watched by the ladies at the Macy's cosmetics counter, and the ladies at the library, and the one male librarian with the long ponytail. They knew her face and expected some kind of interaction, an exchange. So, although she liked the things she found there, she was often relieved when it was not the time for Secret Treasure.

The Bargain Box used an ever-changing collection of delinquent teens to hang the donated clothes on the hangers and load the big shopping cart full of cast-off shoes and put them on the shelves according to size. The teens looked at her, but they did not watch her. Sometimes they looked at her cheerfully, a busy, scouting glance, and sometimes they looked at her sadly, with shame in their eyes and the weariness of old people. A large woman with red cheeks and brown hair in a braid bossed them around. The teens were sent to the Bargain Box by the Municipal Youth Drug Court to perform community service. One of the teens, a friendly boy with floppy hair and pants drooping way down to expose his underwear, tried to explain this to a patron one day, a barrel-chested man who shouted when he talked and had difficulty tracking his eyes and was called by his first name, Jack, by the red-cheeked boss lady. "How come *you* work here?" Jack bellowed to the boy. It was unclear why he was asking the question, if he was dissatisfied with something or just recognized the incongruity between the sleepy, scraggly youth and the bossy woman with the braid. Jack would do that, he would shuffle along in his own world oblivious to his surroundings and then suddenly fixate on someone and want their full engagement. "How come your pants is falling off?" Jack asked a follow-up question now, before the boy had a chance to answer fully the first. "You have a lot of work to do!" Jack exclaimed, pointing at the shopping basket full of shoes waiting to be shelved. The floppy-haired boy just smiled then and kept quiet, having figured out Jack.

She didn't know if these delinquent teens were at risk, like the at-risk youth who lived in the Youth Home. Most of them seemed at play, as they gathered together the shoes and tossed them onto the shelves. There might be two of them, and then they would banter, sometimes saying, "Fuck you!" and using other language not so polite. But not if the boss lady was anywhere near. They yawned and scratched themselves and smiled. They seemed at play, but quietly desperate for their shift to end so they could get out of the windowless building and careen down the street.

~

26.

Jack ambled off in the direction of the Group Home. She finished her shopping, her bargain secreted away in her satchel. Her bargain was another, smaller bag, made from red plastic webbing. Perfectly new, it looked to be. 75 cents. Probably it had come free with an expensive purchase of cosmetics at the Macy's counter.

Heading back to the river front trail, she followed Jack, keeping a distance, matching her pace to suit his, slow and erratic. She didn't want to pass him and have to engage in eye contact or receive a shouted question. He wavered in his direction, sometimes abruptly veering across the road, as if intending to head down an alley or go up to one of the few ramshackle houses that abutted winding California Street. But then he would turn back, just as abruptly, as if obeying orders in his head, and continue along the left hand side of the road, keeping his course straight for a while in the narrow strip of gravel at the asphalt's edge.

She felt the car before she heard it, and she heard it before she saw it. She felt, then heard, the low throb of its chant. *Motherfucker, motherfucker, motherfucker . . .*

She had heard this kind of music before from behind the door of #1B.

When it appeared, the car was going fast and its course was jerky and jig-jagged. Just like Jack's.

~

27.

Jack's big body bounced against the hood and she heard the crack of his head on the windshield before he slid off and into the weeds along California Street. The car plunged briefly into the weeds too, fishtailing, and for a quick moment she saw the driver looking right at her and she heard his shout of "Fuck-*Damn!*" There were others in the car, she heard a girl's high-pitched squeal. She pressed herself up against a shed that bore a sign, TJ Welding, a business that never seemed to be open.

The car roared away, up past the Bargain Box, then left, past the Sister Agatha Shea Center, leaving a smell of burning oil, then silence. Jack lay in the weeds, motionless. His head was thrown back and his arms and legs were flung wide, as if he were making a snow angel in the leaves. She stared at him, waiting for him to shake himself awake. The weeds stirred in the faint breeze. The sky was turning pale violet, the afternoon dusk. She smelled wood smoke. One dry leaf clattered up against the door of TJ Welding and across her shoes.

Again, she felt it before she heard it. Heard it before she saw it. *Motherfucker, motherfucker, motherfucker...* The car was coming back. Up past the Sister Agatha Shea Center, and again, it was coming fast. Her hand fumbled at the doorknob to TJ Welding, but it was locked. She slipped around the side of the building into a new angle of afternoon shadow and fell halfway down a sheltered set of steps into a musty well full of leaves and stacked bricks and sodden newspaper. The car was quiet now, stopped in the street. She heard hissing whispers and yelps. *Jesus Christ! Jesus Fucking Christ!* They were looking at Jack. She heard the voice, the voice she knew. #1B. *Pile 'em on, move it!* the voice barked, and there was a hurried rustling of leaves. Then doors slammed and the engine revved. The car cruised slowly down the street, like a patrol, everyone inside looking.

~

IV.

THE SMELL

28.

There had been five pedestrian deaths in the town in the past two years, three at the zebra crossing on Broadway that motorists completely disregarded. The zebra crossing was at the point where motorists broke free of downtown and zipped toward the big box stores. A crosswalk on this stretch of road, the lone person wanting to cross, simply did not register.

"They act like they have till a week from Tuesday to get across," said Dirk, only he said "acrosst."

And the people who waited to cross were odd, anyway, though no one wanted to say that out loud at any city council meeting. Imagine if someone were to say that out loud: The reason drivers don't stop here—when they stop elsewhere, such as near grade schools, or in the business district, or over by the university—is that the people waiting to cross here are odd, they don't register as legitimate pedestrians with any good reason to go anywhere. They are mostly lumpish bodies on slow, three-wheeled bicycles, or in wheelchairs, some motorized, some not. What if the laboriously driven bicycles or wheelchairs were to get stalled midway across, or what if an occupant simply stopped there, after crossing three lanes, three more to go? Would the waiting motorist have to get out and push? Better to zip on by, pretend you don't see. Let someone else stop, someone who isn't running late.

And sometimes the pedestrians were drunk, plain and simple. These would be the standing pedestrians. The Incorrigibles. They had an official social services designation. They would amble in front of the waiting cars at a leisurely pace, squinting into the windshields' glare to see if they could make out the occupants inside. Or they would be staked out. Staring at you from the curb, with their hand-scrawled sign. Out of work VET. Please help.

"They should try the humane society," Dirk said. "Put in some hours, volunteer type thing, some paid, some in-kind."

"Not that kind of vet!!" she and Sammy had chorused together, that one time, Dirk claiming he was kidding, waving at them with his fork to calm down.

He could see both sides of the crosswalk issue, which was always coming up at city council meetings. A stoplight was proposed. But would it guarantee safety? Orange vinyl flags were provided, they were clustered in buckets on each side of the road. Pedestrians, whether standing or seated in their wheelchairs, some motorized, some not, were to grab a flag and wave it vigorously as they crossed. Wheeling with one hand if not motorized, wheeling and waving.

Were these effective, the flags? Six of one and half a dozen of another. They always disappeared and had to be replaced. Vandals. Teenagers. Driving like bumper cars at the fair, chasing each other down alleys in their parents' cars, or in their new Toyota Tundras, the ink on their learner's permits barely dry, the "adult" from whom they were supposed to be learning someone's older brother. Dirk had followed the discussion. Teenagers took traffic cones, too, or the vandals did, who were probably teenagers, this was documented, so they probably took the flags. But so what anyway, what if more pedestrians or wheelchair people wanted to go from one side to the other than wanted to go back again? Even if all the flags were in place in the buckets, they still would end up all on one side, and then what? There was much discussion. Apples and oranges, someone said. Think outside the box.

Then there were the recent abductions, in daylight hours. Not here, true, but there were some features on TV about it, on *America's Most Wanted*. People posing as handicapped, panhandlers and what-not. Maybe the vagrant pedestrians were posers. Not wheelchair-bound at all. Maybe they would get halfway across the intersection and then leap out of the wheelchair, right into the passenger seat of your car.

"A tip from Tae Kwon Do," said the local news gal, when reporting the rumors of a nationwide trend. "The elbow is the strongest point on your body. Use it!"

The local news gal sat between the sports guy and the weatherman at the end of the half hour. She pretended to elbow the weatherman, and they all three laughed.

~

29.

Alex wasn't the only kid from the neighborhood to enlist. Three doors down, Seth Greenough joined the Marines soon after the news came about Alex. Seth did it to piss off his parents. His parents were the Greeley-Greenoughs, Sara and Pete, co-owners of Eco-Emu and co-presidents of the Butler Creek Neighborhood Association. They were on a lifelong campaign to get others to do right in terms of the environment and neighborhoods and the world and so on. Sara had her WIM thing, a sort of protest coalition. Organized mourning. A grief policy, translated to action. Seth sneered at a lot of things, but he really sneered at that. Seth was into death, in a weird way, skulls and whatnot, but he also didn't approve of it. His enlisting was for the piss-off potential, and it was his own kind of statement about everything, about all this shit, really messed up stuff, goddam fucked up stuff. When he tried to explain it he got incoherent.

Peter Greenough was occasionally at city council meetings referencing Eco-Emu, Dirk said, but he couldn't say what exactly Eco-Emu was, even after Peter told him. It had to do with emus. The Greeley-Greenoughs kept some on their property out of town. Why? said Sammy. They harvested their oil. What? How? Dirk didn't know and didn't want to know.

Sara had very long gray hair, almost past her waist. She wore it flowing. Sammy said he thought it made her look like a Viking.

"She oughta carry one of those hatchets," Sammy said. "Hatchets?" Dirk said. "Yeah, or a cross axe, whatever you call it," said Sammy. "You mean a broad sword?" asked Dirk. "A *broad* sword?" Sammy said. "A *what* sword?"

You just had to close the door to this kind of conversational exchange. You just had to shut yourself up in your kitchen with your little dog who couldn't talk. A "conversational exchange" is what the parenting counselor told her she and Dirk needed to use to engage Sammy. They could model it themselves, the counselor suggested, if Sammy wasn't forthcoming. But Sammy was forthcoming, he came forth plenty, sometimes more than they could stand, or else it was disturbing. Talking about douchebags. Calling Clark a little bitch. Saying, "Welcome to my crib!" when anyone walked into his room with laundry. Obsessing about music groups with names in questionable taste, like Wet Dream. Lately more and more, with the forthcoming, then there would be outbursts. Anger. Irritability. Kicking Clark, or at least threatening with his foot.

Most parents in their peer group took their kids to counselors. It was a Sunnyside thing. Sammy and his fellow alumni all went to counselors now. Or the parents did. Sometimes it was a tag team thing; the parents went for the pre-counseling before the kid went for the counseling. It was what you did these days, post-Sunnyside.

Sammy didn't have a world view, they told the counselor, who said, "Well . . ." Sammy was aimless, they said, and the counselor said, "I see." When Dirk was Sammy's age he sold magazine subscriptions door to door and to his mom. Until he got pants. "Got pants?" said the counselor.

"Yeah, pants, you know, they take them off and throw them in a tree," said Dirk.

"Pantsed," she said. "You got pantsed."

"I know," said Dirk, looking suddenly unhappy.

"Pick a topic with a worldly theme and then stage a mini 'argument' between the two of you," the counselor suggested, "so that there is an exchange of ideas, modeled in conversation."

"How about I just swat his butt?" She had attempted levity. The counselor looked confused, and, glancing at Dirk, a bit alarmed.

"Sammy's," she said. "Sammy's butt."

Dirk was gazing out the window now. He didn't look like anything.

~

30.

The Big thing, Sammy calling Alex his "Big," that was from Sunnyside. She learned that way later, by reading Alex's obituary, which referenced his early days and the Sunnyside system of mentoring. Alex, as one of the primary students, the Minnows, had been a cooperative play mentor for Sammy's preschool circle, who were supposed to be called the Hatchlings, like in a fish nursery, but instead held a vote and changed their name to the Sharks, like in *West Side Story*. She never had been much on going to the parent meetings, so the Big thing had escaped her, and Dirk, who did attend the meetings, sucked at reporting. (She caught herself saying "suck" now, all the time, influenced, no doubt, by Sammy.)

Sammy idolized Seth Greenough almost as much as he'd idolized Alex. Seth had gone to Sunnyside, too, and, in his case, was empowered at an early age to become a badass, a mean, tattooed kid who curled his pierced lip at his parents' eco this 'n that's. They kicked him out of the house. So he enlisted. Off on the train, it's how it went from their hinterland town. Flying was an option, of course, but enlistees always seemed to go off on the train, maybe the local recruiters arranged it for the photo op, part of the nostalgic Greatest Generation thing, Young Men in Uniform. (Never mind the Older Reservists in Uniform, some well into middle age, and/or the Young Gals in Uniform, mothers even, kids left behind, even nursing babies.)

Sammy rode his skateboard down for Seth's send-off, girls crying, their black mascara running all over their ghostly-white cheeks, Seth grinning and wiggling his thumbs and baby fingers like a hip hop artist. He wouldn't do his chores, is what Peter told Dirk. He didn't contribute his own efforts to the household. "Chores?" Dirk responded. Then he tried to cover by saying that Sammy wouldn't do his chores either, not most of the time.

~

31.

The WIM women stood out on the Monroe Bridge downtown every first Tuesday of the month to protest the war in Iraq. Having Seth enlist was for his mother, Sara Greeley-Greenough, like having him join some depraved cult, like going off to Jonestown to drink the Kool-Aid. She'd thought as much about Alex's enlistment, but she didn't want to mention it at the time.

Now Alex was gone, and little Alexis was gone, too, off to live with Celeste, since Ellen was gone. Coach Murphy couldn't take care of little Alexis. He could barely make his own breakfast. He loved little Alexis, but she hadn't really been part of the game plan. She was a surprise, a middle age surprise, just at the time in a person's life when you don't really feel like having a surprise. Celeste, on the other hand, had taken on Alexis as a project, for the time being, a perimenopausal program for staying young. You could see them out mall-walking together, Celeste striding along in her white Nikes, her cheeks flushed, Alexis following anxiously at a toddler's run.

Coach Murphy had gone back to just having basketball players and ex-basketball players around the house now, thirty-somethings who came over and shot hoops in the driveway, self-consciously, like they were being filmed for a life insurance ad.

The dog, crazy Cartman, was gone, disappeared, no one knew where, and Murph wasn't saying.

Coach Murphy commiserated with Sara about it a bit, about Seth enlisting and all, seeing how it was. Sara and the Coach stood out on the sidewalk one day after he had finished his hosing and he said, "Tough." He shook his head and looked mournful so that it sounded sympathetic, not belligerent. That's all he could pull up, but Sara said she appreciated it, knowing how gung-ho he was about everything violent. Despite all. Sara said this later to Dirk when they got to talking out on the street, and Dirk then passed it along at The Family Meal, which oftentimes was just two adults plus Clark.

"Seth gets to go to Hawaii," Sammy reported later. Yeah, yeah, he knew, Alex had thought so too. But Seth'd swing it.

Soon after, Sara told them that Seth had not gone to Hawaii at all. Instead, he was stationed on Guam and was learning to surf.

~

32.

Something smelled funny in the house. Not bad, just funny. The same funny smell. She was thinking about that smell while she was raking up the last of the leaves, trying to ignore Coach Murphy, who was again wielding his leaf blower like a seismograph. A big strong man like that, you'd think he'd want some exercise. Instead he stood there in his sweatshirt like something mechanical, keeping the arc of his arm exactly uniform, back and forth, back and forth. Some of the leaves he was blowing were skittering in her direction. She swatted them back.

After he finished up and stowed away his toy and did his stretches and stared at the skateboard ramps, he ambled on over across the street. Damn. The man was not exactly a genius at conversational exchange. She would have to think up sentences for him to respond to after his inevitable "How's life treatin' ya?" He would stand there with his hands in his pockets waiting for her to deal with him. He was used to Ellen managing him. But Ellen left no instructions for Coach Murphy's management, and no instructions for Alexis's care, although, before she died, she did manage to convert not only her wardrobe, but also her bicycle and even the mailbox to Pepto-Bismol pink.

She definitely sensed that Coach Murphy wanted her to manage him, on some level. She might say "Fine," when Coach Murphy came across the street and asked her how life was treating her, but he wouldn't let her just leave it at that. Ever since Ellen, he'd wait in anticipation, like he was Clark. Probably he wanted her to feed him. Sara Greeley-Greenough was always feeding Coach Murphy, carrying covered hot dishes up the street, stuff like polenta and baba ghanoush. He barely recognized it as food, but he ate it all, Sara said, or at least he returned the dish clean.

Today, though, was a surprise. After his "How's life treatin' ya?" and after her "Fine," he actually said something else, with no encouragement at all.

"See you got yourself a cleaning gal," is what he said. "So how's that working out for ya?"

"Oh, well . . . fine."

It popped out of her mouth like that because to say "What cleaning gal?" would provide an opening, plus she didn't know what he was talking about. Probably it was just Sammy's friend Walt. The last time she'd seen Walt, Sammy's friend since fourth grade, his hair had grown into flowing locks and he was wearing a cape. A "tween" thing, no doubt. Except he and Sammy were post-tween. At thirteen and a half they were tween veterans, fully established future citizens, to use Dirk's terminology.

"Citizens of the planet WD-40's second lunar moon!" Sammy might have said up until recently. "Betwixt and between. Visible only during a copolypleptic event, a planetary breakdown!"

Walt talk.

Now Sammy might start going off on the lunar moon, then suddenly switch, turn a corner. Rearrange his face. Deepen his voice, open the refrigerator and gaze in, rolling his head in a half circle, spreading his legs like his falling down pants were shackles, saying, "What the fuck," apropos of nothing. She'd tried fining him. Ten cents for "shit," a quarter for "fuck." For a while that worked, but then Sammy would say he didn't have the cash and she'd make him write her an I.O.U. And then she'd just forget about it.

"The mailman cometh."

An odd thing to come out of Coach Murphy's mouth.

"Afternoon."

The mailman performed his hand off. She tucked the rake under her arm and shuffled through the mail quickly, as if she had been waiting for something. Then she abruptly threw the rake onto her token pile of leaves and, waving a catalog at Coach Murphy, hastened up her sidewalk and through the front door.

~

33.

Sometimes she overpaid bills so that she would get a refund. It was a way to regain the pleasurable thrill she had felt once in Dirk and her early days, when they'd been pretty much broke, and she had mistakenly paid O'Hara Heating twice for a furnace inspection and one day found a refund check in the mail. She and Dirk had been reduced to looking in the sofa for spare change during that particular era, or rummaging through their off-season coat pockets, so the check was a great boon. Now Dirk made good money and wouldn't know if it went to pay O'Hara Heating or Osama Bin Laden, so she didn't know why she sometimes overpaid or double paid bills to get a refund. It was a financial wash, so big deal. She just liked getting a check in the mail.

Today she got no refund checks, but she did get a book from Amazon. It was something she'd ordered after overhearing some talk at yoga about wellness décor while sitting on her mat in the lotus position waiting for the session to begin. *Feng Shui: Cure Your Ills.* She sat down in the hunting hound chair and flipped it open.

Can you imagine waking each morning and steering your sleepy self up a slanting floor to reach your first cup of coffee? Starting off each day facing an upward slope might, over time, make you dread getting up.

She figured she'd better hide this from Dirk.

She rose to close the drapes against Coach Murphy's stretching and stares and caught sight of Sammy coming up the walk on his longboard, his skateboard that was an accommodating size for his big shoes, banana shaped with fat wheels, a simple mode of transportation, no tricks. She hurriedly shoved the book on top of the others in the bookcase and pushed it back so that *Feng Shui* would be safely out of sight.

~

34.

For some reason Clark had taken to barking at members of the family. Just as soon as they got in the front door he'd go wild. He would sit quietly until then, his eyes fixed on the door. Right when he saw their faces, he'd begin—a piercing staccato yip, regular as a metronome.

"Thirteen years living with us and he starts doing this," said Dirk. Thirteen was too old to put him in the Go Fetch van, she thought, but that's what Dirk wanted to do. Every week poor Clark would have to run around in the woods with young Golden Retrievers, trying to keep up on his arthritic little legs. By this move, by rifling through the Yellow Pages in an irritated manner, Dirk was really saying she should walk Clark every day, put on his leash and maybe even put on his little sweater. And by tacitly suggesting that, what he was really saying was that she had nothing better to do and that his time was more valuable than hers. Sometimes a whole conversational exchange could take place in practically stone cold silence.

She might respond with a little distracting fear mongering, knowing this would punch Dirk's buttons, she'd bring up tidbits of urban lore sent to her by her father, via email.

"This neighborhood is getting so totally quiet these days," she might say. "All the little kids growing up, going away..." (Dying. She didn't say that.)

"I read that if you are ever thrown into the trunk of a car, you should kick out the back tail lights and stick your arm out the hole and start waving like crazy. The driver won't see you, but everybody else will."

This time she was thinking about running a relaxing bath as Dirk flipped through the phone book looking for Go Fetch, so she merely stated: "He's old."

But she felt that if she and Dirk lived in another era, one of corsets and cooks and evening talks by the fire, they would be forced to explore the tense, layered implications in Dirk's insistence on Go Fetch.

"Fifteen bucks a week, big deal," said Dirk to himself, feeding Clark another dog biscuit to shut him up.

~

35.

A letter from her father, just a note, with a print-out of an email he already had sent her, as if he felt that its seriousness could not be adequately conveyed other than by hard copy. Or maybe he'd just forgotten that he'd sent it.

Fw: Life saving tips. THIS IS BEING FORWARDED AND SHARED FOR THE OBVIOUS REASON(S). REMINDER: As it mentions below, it's safer to be PARANOID AND ALIVE than the alternative . . . Thirty years ago a young lady who worked with me at the naval air station, Pensacola, had #4 below happen to her, only the abductor's weapon was a knife instead of a gun. Please be EXTRA VIGILANT while out and about shopping etc. Love, Pa.

These emails, two or three a year, had started arriving after 9/11, the Twin Towers. Ordinary life turned disastrous on a dime. This had become a fixation for her father. She skimmed to #4. As usual, her father's computer printed online stuff funny.

4. Women have a tendency to get into their
cars
after shopping, eating, working, etc., and
just sit
(doing their checkbook, making a list, etc.)
(DON'T DO THIS!)

The predator will be watching you, and this is
the perfect opportunity for him
     to get in on the passenger side,
     put a gun to your

                              head,

     and tell you where to go.

                    ~

36.

She'd seen it when she hid the *Feng Shui* book, but it hadn't really registered. Something, not a book, tucked way back in the bookcase. Only later, when she and Dirk were watching all the flooding on CNN, did she suddenly think of it.

"Gone, all gone," a distraught flood victim sobbed through an interview. She sobbed in Spanish and a voice-over translated. Hurricane Katrina was now Hurricane Wilma and New Orleans had become Cozumel.

Next there was a beer commercial that showed a couple at the beach under a colorful umbrella, contemplating a placid sea. Watching the couple with their beach accessories made her think of the little orange and pink makeup bag, *Estee Lauder* BEAUTY, tucked way back in the bookcase. She had the bigger tote version, free for buying a small fortune's worth of anti-aging cream with moisture technology for the reconstruction and rehabilitation and soothing of her skin.

She got up and walked out to the kitchen, opening the refrigerator door and staring inside, then closing it. Then she walked to the living room and stared at the little orange and pink makeup bag. Just the edge was visible, next to *It*, one of the few books she knew for sure that Sammy had read. She knew because she had paid him $25 to read it and made him take a quiz of her devising. (*Question:* What was the scary guy dressed up like? *Answer:* A clown.*)* Books made into horror movies, the only genre that really inspired Sammy's artistic passion, got $25, books made out of horror movies, $10.

She could hear Sammy upstairs in his bedroom jumping on his skateboard. He stood on the board right there on his King Kong rug and leapt up into the air and slammed down hard. It was nerve wracking, but at least he was in the house, so she didn't yell. So much lately he was not. He was off on his longboard until all hours, Dirk was off to meetings, she was left with Clark. She and Clark would turn on the TV and watch *America's Most Wanted*, which made the dark outside even darker, so then they'd switch to *Friends*, by mutual consent.

She looked at the bag and had a bad feeling. Once last year she had snooped through Sammy's backpack—some of the parenting books said you should do that with middle-schoolers—and found two plastic prescription containers. Inside were little buds of pot. The prescriptions were for Tylenol 3, the kind with codeine, but there were no pills, just the pot. She had Lorazepam around the house, but no Tylenol 3. Plus the prescription containers had someone else's name on them, Carly something, no one she'd ever heard of. She put the containers back in Sammy's backpack and went around for a week feeling sick. She knew she should sit Sammy down and say, "What's up with this?" That's how she would say it, she even practiced it. But she didn't sit Sammy down and she never mentioned the incident to Dirk, who didn't favor snooping. She had thought she might mention it to Ellen at the time, because Ellen knew about medicinal pot and whatnot, but then there was the news about Alex, and then Ellen started opting out, and then Ellen was gone.

She pushed the bag in a little with her finger so it hardly showed at all. She didn't know if she wanted to see inside the bag. She went back to watching the flooding on CNN. Sandbags passed from hand to hand, disembodied arms outstretched in a pouring rain, a man sloshing through water with a child clinging to his back, pulling the child's hands off his eyes so he could see where he was going.

She thought about stuff, all the stuff going on, Clark's maintenance, Coach Murphy's management, Sammy's increasing absence, Dirk's sinus infections and stomach complaints, coming up with some frequency of late. The total, absolute absence of Ellen, like a dark night with no moon.

Alex had gone off on the train, and then he'd gone off to Iraq and come back dead. It was awful but it was something that happened. (You didn't expect it to happen now in the modern world, though, the world where war was obsolete, at least per the signage.) But Ellen. Ellen died of *sickness*. Avoidable, you felt. A big, big mistake. Ellen was her age, or even a little bit younger. Ellen was the mother of a little girl, little Alexis, and she had just *left* her, abandoned her, gone off forever, no longer a factor, X'ed out of the equation. She and Ellen hadn't been super close, but still. How could she disappear?

She lapsed into the vague, sad crankiness and anxious irritability that she used to blame on PMS, but now it was life. Sally Field was being especially annoying this evening in the osteoporosis ads.

"Hiya girlfriend!" Sally Field said with her eyes, but you knew she was in it for the money.

~

37.

The mention of a cleaning lady, or cleaning "gal," as Coach Murphy said it, made her realize that she did want a cleaning lady, a gal, someone to come and pull things together here, dust a little, walk Clark, dig out Sammy's room, maybe get something cooking. She herself could come back to the house from yoga class or Pilates class or Target and the house would smell like dinner. She could be like a school kid again, walking in the door, someone thinking about her for a change, her needs, her health, her hunger.

She almost started to ask Coach Murphy one day where he got his cleaning gal. She actually started across the street while he was out methodically putting some kind of defreezer on his sidewalks, even though there was nothing to defreeze, the air being damply cold but the sidewalks bare because of global warming, which Coach Murphy had not yet heard about. She started to head across the street on her way from the car to her front door, and then she remembered that he had been the one to ask her about a cleaning lady, not the other way around, he had said, "I see you have a cleaning gal," which she didn't have but now wanted. She had meant to think more about that, about why Coach Murphy thought she had a cleaning gal, it had been on her To Think About list, along with the little plaid bag in the bookshelves and the traffic cones on Sammy's lower bunk and a number of other things that she couldn't think of right now.

~

When she did sit down to think, she decided she'd better focus on Walt. Walt was usually the source. Walt had become Sammy's very best friend when Sammy transferred at fourth grade from Sunnyside—a "parent-cooperative, secular humanist learning center for grades Pre to 3"—into the public system. Sammy's other Sunnyside cohorts went on to Derbyshire, billed as a "progressive preparatory academy for children, young adults, and their communities of support." "Parent" had been left off the Derbyshire description after much debate about definitions of family, but there were still parent hours required, or "support hours," and Dirk was too involved with city council now to do all that, and she had heard anyway that the Derbyshire kids ate psychedelic mushrooms on field trips to Guatemala. (They did, Sara G-G confirmed, but only nibbles, and only supervised.)

Walt was a source of information, often given inadvertently, a source of jokes, a source of trouble. Walt had not attended Sunnyside. Walt had attended a number of public schools from the age of five on, all over town, usually transferring mid-year when his Mom had to move because she couldn't make the rent or pay the phone bill.

Sammy had been fearful of going to Butler School, hearing that kids ate rocks on the school bus, so she had been fearful, too. (They did, she later learned from Sammy, who said one kid choked and threw up.) Dirk had been dismissive of their fear. The real problem with the buses, according to Dirk, was the seatbelt issue. The buses oughta have them, and the kids oughta wear them, but then if they did they might horse around and get hung up and strangle. Only one bus driver, with one set of eyes, and not in the back of his head. But who would drive Sammy all the livelong day, if the bus was out?

Clark, obviously, didn't care. He waited with the same butt-wiggling anticipation for Sammy to come home no matter where Sammy went. He didn't look at Sammy anxiously to see if the broader world was effecting a change. He didn't sniff at Sammy's backpack, unless it contained rotten food, which sometimes was the case, a salmonella-ridden tuna fish sandwich maybe, several days old. He didn't worry about Sammy's grades and bribe him with promises to rent horror movies to entice him toward A's. Clark did none of that. Sammy, to Clark, was just Sammy, one-of-a-kind, perfect and complete. That was the case, at least, until Clark started losing it, as he had of late, barking at them all as if they were strangers.

She was happy the day that Sammy came home from school—after several weeks of moping and having stomach aches and dreading the bus—and said that he had made a new friend, Walt. He and Walt, Sammy reported, spent the recess period and lunchtime picking grass at the edges of the playground with their bare hands, calling it straw and stuffing it under their shirts, like the Scarecrow in *The Wizard of Oz*. They did this all through fourth grade, then, in fifth grade, the game changed. She got a call from the principal, who was concerned about violent expression. Columbine, the telltale signs; the principal had attended a seminar. Sammy and Walt, the principal reported, after stuffing their shirts, would "shoot" each other with sticks, and, victims both, yank out big handfuls of the grass, spewing it all over, the Scarecrow's straw transformed into innards and blood. Then they'd gather the grass back up again, re-stuff their shirts, and start in again shooting.

At Sunnyside they had played cooperative games, the big kids mentoring the little ones. Now it was grass guts, all over the place. But she was glad that Sammy had a public school friend, and when Sammy called from Walt's house to see if he could hang out there until dinnertime, she said sure, and when he asked to spend the

night there, she said okay, and when he started spending both week-
end nights there—so that sometimes they didn't see him from Friday
morning until Sunday night—she said to Dirk: I'm glad Sammy has
a friend.

~

38.

She went to Target. She had to wait at the crossing for the train. The day trains came at 12:30, at 4, and again at 6:30. Right when people needed to cross. You'd think they'd make an overpass. All the big Suburbans, lined up, waiting to go to yoga class, to Pilates, to Stressbusters. Waiting to get home from work.

The cars were stopped, spewing exhaust. Doors were locked. (*The predator will be watching you...*) The collective impatience of the cars could be felt, the big Suburbans and the Broncos and the Cherokees. Some would inch forward, nose their neighbor. Some would pull to the side, to get a better look. The Hummers hummed. Fingers tapped, cell phones snapped open. Necks were stretched. The necks were stretched from side to side, loosening up. NPR was turned on, then off. The news was disturbing. Al Qaeda. Hostage situations. iPods were engaged, CDs were found, they were pushed in and then they were played, the mind encouraged to disengage itself from the boredom and discomfort that the body was experiencing.

~

"Capitation," Dirk called it. Another capitation.

"Decapitation," she said.

"I know," he replied. "What I said."
It was the insurgents and the mercy-naries.

~

39.

She lay flat, awake. She didn't know why. Some nights she was just awake, listening, her eyes wide, watching the world from the tangled confines of her bed. Listening to Dirk, wheezing. He wheezed in rhythm, but it still kept her awake. The room was bright; it was the street light, it was on too bright. No, not the street light, the moon. The moon, floating high overhead, watching her, solemn, expectant, unsmiling.

Oh my god, she hated insomnia.

She tried the relaxation trick. My forehead is relaxed, she silently recited, the muscles of my forehead, relaxed. The bridge of my nose, relaxed. My cheek muscles are relaxed and the muscles of my mouth, relaxed. My neck is relaxed. And my shoulders. My arms are both relaxed. The muscles of my stomach, relaxed.

She always stopped there.

Dirk wheezed.

He had been excited at dinner about that day's city council meeting. They'd discussed the crosswalk problem, again, same old thing. And people taking shortcuts up California Street, going too fast, that retarded guy killed, probably hit 'n run.

"Disabled," she said.

"What?" said Dirk.

"That guy was disabled."

"Yeah, I know."

The poor disabled guy, his body found when burning leaves nearly torched a neighborhood. A dry fall, windy. The forest fires of the summer had died down with the cooler weather, the big slurry bombers that dropped the retardant were parked for the winter. But little spot fires still popped up here and there, even in town. Could be arson, or cinders from a smoking woodstove, or kids playing with matches. As yet undetermined.

But Dirk didn't want to talk about the alleged hit 'n run or the town fire—that was old news. The new news was a proposed expansion of a neighborhood school, Sunnyside School, as a matter of fact. Dirk used to like going to all those parent meetings when Sammy was at Sunnyside, before they both went on to broader arenas. He had argued about many things. The parking lot puddles. The "right turn only" sign, to decrease "congestion," as he put it. She noticed that the Greeley-Greenoughs smiled when Dirk was being serious. This made her pretend to sit up and take notice, listen more closely than she was accustomed to doing in the privacy of the home, engage in Dirk's discourse at the Butler Creek Neighborhood Association meetings, the ice cream socials with agendas, standing there with the Greeley-Greenoughs under a porta-tent, eating a tofu hot dog she didn't want, 10% going to support new bubble curbs or whatever, some extension of the sidewalks at the Butler Creek intersections to slow down the traffic that rarely came.

Dirk used to rehash those Sunnyside parent meetings *ad nauseam*. He'd pick fights and create enmities and go around the house whistling. Now Sammy's education was administered by the tedious and cumbersome public realm and the school board meetings droned on about trees on the playground (Did they promote illicit drug use at recess?) and cars at schools (Could all those overgrown 8th grade boys who were held back in kindergarten, per the thinking of then, drive *themselves* to school now?). But the trustees looked pale and aged on Community Access TV and had less power, overall, than the City Council members, or so Dirk decided. He weighed the question of the allocation of his time at some length over dinner more than once, she and Clark attempting to look engaged and interested, Sammy again gone off somewhere. City Council meetings won the battle for Dirk's heart and mind. And now the avocations of his life were coming together—he was thinking of challenging the Sunnyside proposed expansion. Neighborhood congestation. Vagrant workers passing through. Noise levels at recess time. Too many kids shrieking their lungs out. He thought he might rent one of those altimeters, or whatever, those things that measure cacophony.

"Measure what?" she asked.

"Noise, noise," Dirk said.

The school was seven blocks from their house, she pointed out. Their street was morgue-like in its silence. She pointed that out, too.

~

40.

A uniform at the door, just like when Ellen heard about Alex. Only this was a regular old policeman, not a military type. And she didn't have anyone in the military to get news about. Sammy was only thirteen. Sammy was at school.

But there he was, a tall policeman, his hat looking oversized, like a Halloween costume hat, a Halloween policeman. She tried to make her mouth quit wiggling into a grin as she listened to him talk out there on the stoop with Clark going berserk. Clark sniffed the policeman's pants in between yaps and something that he smelled made him flip, literally. He flipped backwards into the bushes. Then he shook himself, ran in a large circle that encompassed the front lawn and half the street, then resumed his barking and sniffing.

Coach Murphy took in everything, rake in hand.

Yes, she was Sammy's mother. She nodded her head as if she'd just fathomed the answer to a problem. She certainly was, she was Sammy's mother. Sammy wasn't home.

He was at school. At school.

~

41.

Sammy's punishment was to clean. He was Cleaning Gal for a Day, she said, handing him the yellow rubber gloves, a bucket, the bleach, all of it. A mascara wand for getting at scum hiding in tiny cracks and crevices, a tip from *Get Simple*. She was not at all sure she would be able to make him do anything. Skipping school, stealing beer, vandalizing property, and who knew what else? "Better'n community service, huh?" she said. "Better'n working at the Goodwill or whatever, eh?" The officer hadn't been a regular officer, he'd been a PROS officer, Police-Responsible-Others-Safety, something like that, a school policeman.

She tickled Sammy's nose with a feather duster, trying for a buddy-buddy thing. He said, "Fuck this," and dumped the cleaning supplies in the middle of the kitchen floor, making Clark yelp when the bucket bounced onto his Posh Dog Pet Bed. He dumped the supplies and left out the back door, not even bothering to slam it, just marched right out and slapped down his longboard and down the street he went, right past Dirk driving up.

She thought about crying, but didn't, because she wanted to minimize it. All this stuff going on, all of it, this stuff, she wanted to minimize it to Dirk in order to spare her and Clark's ears all through dinner.

"Where's Sammy going?" Dirk asked, "What are you doing?"

"Cleaning," she said.

"Duh," said Dirk.

She went at the grout with the mascara wand, her hand jittering along, all the cleaning supplies clustered around her on the kitchen floor.

"Coughs and sneezes spread diseases," she said, when Dirk went into his pre-dinner hacking routine. It was like he stored up all his respiratory combustion until he got into the house, where he could explode in comfort. He said he thought he was allergic to Clark, after all these years. She said she thought he probably had one of those viruses she'd read about in *Globe and Cosmos*. Pig viruses, bird viruses, desert fever. Maybe chicken leukemia.

He forgot to ask anymore about Sammy.

~

42.

Clark had taken to hiding things. He hid her cell phone, and even though she called and called, there was no answer. Well, there was probably nothing to answer, it probably was on Silent. She probably forgot to turn it back on after yoga class. And then it was gone, and Clark looked guilty. So she had to go down to the Verizon store and wait the requisite seventeen hours while the little girl with the cleavage reprogrammed her a new one. Latest model, state of the art, why the hell not? She got a whole new number because, who knows, the old phone could turn up and, meanwhile, Clark would have stolen this new one. Who cared how big the bill was? Let it grow. She would have two numbers now, one as backup. Why the hell was life so complicated? Why the hell did it always take so much time to get a new cell phone, program it and whatever, the little girl's cleavage looking smudged, as if she had applied foundation makeup to it, the cleavage, a thing unto itself.

All this time not quality.

Clark hid Dirk's John Mellencamp CD, the one he always took with him driving. He hid Sammy's wallet, his canvas wallet from Odyssey Skateshop, hid it good, so Sammy lost his student ID and about sixty dollars. Clark couldn't refund it, obviously, so she did. She glared at Clark while she counted out the twenties, and told him he was going to have to make restitution (relieved, even as she said it, that Dirk wasn't around to make that his word-of-the-day). She told Clark he was going to have to pick up his own poop for five weeks.

She knew it was Clark because she had caught him trotting around the house with something in his mouth not his. Not even. Not his, not anyone's. Not hers, not Dirk's, not Sammy's. How he managed to rip someone off when he hardly ever got out of the house except to do his business in the yard was beyond her. Dirk didn't walk him, Dirk just put the Go Fetch number on the refrigerator, in large print, like a warning. Dirk could use a walk, God knows; he got winded just looking at a set of steps. But Dirk didn't walk him.

Sammy didn't walk him, even when she quickly put Clark's little halter leash on his rubbery neck when she saw Sammy skateboarding up the walk, so that Clark got all excited and wiggled his butt to high heaven when Sammy walked in, thinking Sammy was taking him for a walk, because that's what she said, a bunch of times, "Sammy's coming, Sammy's coming, time for a walk, a walk, a walk with Sammy, with Sammy." Clark would leap at Sammy's pant legs as soon as he saw him. She'd get him so worked up and then Sammy would fling him off like he was an attack rabbit, what they used to watch and laugh at together, those attack rabbits in *Monty Python and the Holy Grail.*

Clark was trotting around the house with a little red tote bag made from lawn furniture webbing, but she really didn't think he'd gnawed up somebody's lawn furniture and then fashioned it into a handbag. No, she really didn't think so. She was trying for humor. Dirk looked away from the TV and blinked at Clark, then turned back to watching Katie Couric. Katie was reporting about the amount of trash gathered annually from things falling off of the backs of trucks on freeways. Enough to fill twelve football fields. Annually.

Clark made that, she said to Sammy, when he looked at Clark's purse.

"It's soggy," Sammy said, with some hostility that she could detect. "It's soggy from his nasty spit."

Normally Sammy would get into it. He'd call Clark a designer dog and ask him to make him stuff, a "man purse" maybe, normally Sammy would call Clark's little handbag a man purse and order one for himself. But nothing was normal now.

~

43.

Pick Up Stix. That was the name of the lawn service. That's what the guy said, and that's what was hand scrawled with a magic marker in black block letters on the pocket of his rumpled coat. Light lawn work, the guy said. Twig retrieval. No lawn mower in sight, no tools, no truck even. He pointed at the twigs from the dying Chinese elm, the one by the driveway, the twigs scattered all over Sammy's skate ramps, blown there by the day's breeze and the previous night's wind, unusual, a high wind scudding the clouds along the sky and knocking down the twigs. Made both her and Dirk sleepless, Dirk guzzling Pepto-Bismol and padding around the house in her own bathrobe and fleece fuzzy-stompers, things he didn't want to own but now needed, being sleepless. He said he felt a premonation. "Of what?" she asked, not bothering to tweak his vowels. "I don't know," he said, "that's what a premonation is, you don't know."

(Water scam! If you wake up in the middle of the
night to hear all your taps
Outside running or what you think is a burst pipe, DO NOT
GO OUT TO INVESTIGATE!
These people
turn on all your outside taps full ball so that you will go out
to investigate
and then they attack. Love, Pa.)

"I can pick up your sticks," the guy at the door said to her, while she held the house phone in her hand, pretending he'd interrupted a call. That's what you should do if the doorbell rings unexpectedly, she'd read in *Get Simple*. For both safety and convenience.

The guy at the door smiled at her with uniform lips, and then they both looked at the twigs and all the junk scattered around, the boards and ramps and blocks stacked up to put things at angles. The skate rail, a heavy metal bar that always tripped Dirk as he came from the driveway. Once Dirk tried to throw it across the yard, but he only succeeded in pulling a muscle in his groin and slightly wounding Clark.

Clark was gone just now, or he'd be going nuts with this twig guy. Clark was on a walk, wonder of wonders. Sammy obliged. She had no idea why, but off they went, about ten minutes ago, Sammy dragging Clark, who wanted to stop and sniff and pee every third step.

She looked at the twigs. She looked at the guy. She looked at his pants, about a yard wide, each leg, and falling down, as they did, she knew they were supposed to do that, she understood, it was the youth culture and the twenty-somethings, it was no big deal. He smelled, not bad, sort of aromatic, like vanilla. Vanilla and mulch. She looked at Coach Murphy Busybody, coming out of his house just then, and the twig guy turned around and looked at him too. Face on, the twig guy looked okay, except for the pants and his bald head and jug ears. But from the back, he looked scary, he had a zigzag tattoo on the back of his shaved head, not cute nor clever, more Frankenstein than Scarecrow.

"No thanks," she said, after hesitating just a bit, and saying "um-hum, um-hum, just a sec" into the phone receiver. "Not today, I guess," she said to the baggy pants smelly twig guy. "Catch you later!" she said, when he said it as he walked away, her matched response super friendly and bright.

~

44.

It was done, she took the bull by the horns, accomplished, a fate accomplice.

"I hired a cleaning gal," she said, waving the flyer she'd found in their door. She told Dirk and Sammy and Clark this, as they had The Family Meal, the at-least-once-a-week prescription from *Get Simple*'s special parenting issue for improved family dynamics. They were all standing. This was not how The Family Meal was depicted in *Get Simple*'s glossy photo spread, where everyone sat at a table with an autumnal theme and smiled at a story told by the little girl at the end of the table, turned in her direction, giving her their full, undivided attention.

She said it, then Sammy spilled his milk all over the breakfast counter bar, where they usually stood or perched on stools, in tandem, having different schedules, eating different "foodstuffs," as Sammy liked to call the various microwave dinners she stuck in the freezer at periodic intervals, the results of random hunting and gathering forays to local supermarkets. Until recently, she and Sammy had both liked to talk this way. Until recently, they'd had that.

"I'm going to forage, then I'll be over," Sammy would stand in the kitchen and say this to his cell phone.

She'd tried planning meals and all that, and sometimes they did have a meal, almost by accident, all three of them together, when their schedules coincided and similar foodstuffs could be found in adequate allotments. The Family Meal was supposed to be something different from this chaotic arrangement, that much she knew. It was supposed to be a sit down time with nourishing dishes and shared stories. She'd been meaning to whack out the breakfast bar with a crowbar or a Saws-All so that they'd be forced to remodel. Then they would have a breakfast nook that could accommodate a little table, and they could sit there and face each other and share. But she hadn't gotten around to it. It was on the list.

No one would clean up the milk. Sammy claimed that the tumbler was tippy, so it wasn't his fault. Dirk concurred, those were tippy tumblers. He looked at her accusingly. She wasn't buying it, and she called Sammy a toddler. Then she called Dirk a toddler. Clark, having finished lapping up the milk on the floor, started barking maniacally, like a toddler dog. She turned on her heel and flipped them all off, she actually did that, Clark included, as she marched up the stairs to get her workout clothes.

Everyone forgot about the cleaning gal. There was no discussing it as a family.

~

45.

On Tuesdays and Thursdays she strengthened her core at the Pilates Palace, on Mondays, Wednesdays, and Fridays she softened her brain at the Yoga Studio, and on Saturdays she went to the university health club and spinned. Riding stationary bikes, all in a group, like they were going somewhere.

"I'm going to go spin," she'd say, and Sammy, when he was just a little bit littler and a little bit sweeter, would shout, "Spin straw into gold!"

~

V.

THE RIVER

46.

It was a good bag for wet things, and she had thought he might find it useful in any number of ways. She sat in the tall chair with the hunting hounds, her hands in her lap. It was a good bag for Eddy's swim trunks and towel after coming out of the locker room at the city pool. She'd be waiting and she'd put the wet things into the bag and they would walk across the park, following their shadows, the pool kids' cries and splashing receding as the sun edged down the length of the cottonwoods.

She looked at the spot in the bookshelves where she had stowed the webbed bag. When he came in the front door and slammed his skateboard down on the hall tile and threw his backpack along with it and shouted, *Hiya Nutwad!* to the little barking dog, and there was a moment of silence and she heard him say, *Yep, yep, good dog, good dog, yer a good dog, yer a good dog, yep, yep,* the little dog's barking now a sweet keen, she thought about the bag she had tucked away for him and she thought about the gift enclosed, the Tootsie Pop and the dollar bill. She could see the *Estee Lauder* plaid bag, the gift from another day, the gift to the house, her house, just that, an offering. It sat there, unmoved. But she could no longer see the edge of the red webbed bag, where she had tucked it in next to a pile of skateboard magazines on the bottom shelf, thinking there he might find it, like finding the Easter egg with the lucky number, or the precious remains of a year's trick-or-treat hoard.

This had happened once before, the boy coming home while she quietly sat hidden in the arms of the hunting hound chair. And that time she also had heard this happy voice and sensed him petting the little dog, so that she had thought there were two boys. She saw the other boy downtown on his skateboard, and that boy said, "Fuck *Damn!*" in a rough voice when his board clattered out of control, nearly hitting her. That boy did not say, "Sorry." He looked right through her as if she weren't there, and she saw his blue eyes up close. That boy glanced quickly at his companions, bigger boys slouched along a wall, watching. They watched the boy on the skateboard, and they watched her, they watched her walking. She was shaken to see #1B in among the bigger boys. His eyes found hers and his fingers tapped his forehead and flicked skyward, a mock salute.

Once she passed the boy on the steep, steel steps by the river. He was coming up alone as she was going down. He was coming up fast, taking the steps two at a time, holding his skateboard, the stairs vibrating and ringing from his clamber. She stopped and clung to the rail and squeezed herself to the edge, but his skateboard still ticked her elbow, and he shouted, "Scuse me! Sorry!" over his shoulder in a high child's voice.

She was glad he had found the bag, the red webbed bag, her gift to him.

She felt the furnace go on and noticed how the warm air stirred the curtains. Her heart shifted. Outside her window the weeping birch was nearly bare. She kept still while he went into the kitchen and looked in the refrigerator, talking on his cell phone, his voice changed now, his voice changed to deep and hoarse, saying, "Whatup? When? No . . . Hey man, I tried. I can't. Just cause. Chillin' at my house. Early out. Why? Sure man, you got it. Hey, no problem. No way! Ok, sweet. Sick. *Sick.* Ok. Later, bro."

And then the phone call ended and there was a moment of quiet and then his voice turned back to that of a child and the high child voice whispered *shit... shit.*

She kept still, counting, *one aw-loo, one aw-loo, one* ... while he climbed the stairs in silence. And then she heard him whistling and slamming cupboard doors. She leaned forward and palmed the silver matches with her gloved hand, slipping them into her satchel, a small gift back. And then she heard him sing a loud WAH-AH! WHA-AH-AH! When she heard the toilet flush, she slipped out the door.

~

47.

#2A was empty. #2B was empty, too. They both had been empty for a long time while Garden Gate Rentals made improvements, or so the tiny man once said, he had hinted at this, the little, leaf-raking man, former #1B, in an awkward Monday morning washing day exchange. She had arrived, he had stepped aside, basket held in both hands. Next in this careful dance he was supposed to move past her, smiling but not speaking, not touching. But he stayed still, the basket held forward a bit, as if he were asking for a donation.

"The building folks sure are fixing things." That is what he said, and he jerked his head upwards to indicate the floors above. Then he coughed dryly and smiled with white lips. "Yes," she said, her own voice faint. But she didn't know if this were true. She ducked her head and performed a sort of curtsy, picking up something invisible from the floor. He moved on out of the room and then, a few weeks later, he moved on for good. She didn't see him go. She just knew that he was gone.

She listened for sounds from above, sounds of the building folks fixing things. The building was empty except for the occupants of #1A—herself—and #1B, the noisy boy who cursed at night. Upstairs was a shell. The building next door, too, was a shell. The downtown was seeping out to the houses and apartments, a river beyond its banks, filling the buildings, then sucking out the occupants and all their belongings.

She heard a door close once, quietly. But she heard no further sounds from #2A. She heard nothing. No sounds of footsteps, no boots on the stairs, no cupboards opening and closing, no chair falling over, no muffled laughter, no angry voices, no pacing, no crying, no sounds, she heard nothing, nothing at all.

She didn't see Audrey walking down the steps one morning, her face averted. Her Audrey. *Audrey aw-loo.* She saw her and she didn't see her. She didn't see her.

~

48.

If her table for two was occupied she stopped in the foyer, just inside the outer door and just outside the inner door, and waited, pretending to read the flyers. Sometimes she actually did read them. There were lost dog flyers with photos of the animal in question, usually a mutt-like creature, maybe shaggy black with white markings, a bandana around the neck, tongue lolling. There were typed advertisements for house cleaners and yard workers. There was the domestic abuse hotline poster, with a photo of a woman with a bowed head, and a phone number in red. There was a tiny house for sale for $179,000. The house was said to have charm and a good location, even if it was on an alley.

Today, there was a flyer about an estate sale. A "Living Estate" sale, it was called. A ninety-year-old (still alive) divesting herself or himself of the possessions of nearly a century. Books, antiques, Christmas decorations, vintage wear, kitchenware, craft items, sheet music, instruments, collectables. Indoors, free coffee.

The street name of the address was her street, where several old houses still remained, chopped up into apartments maybe, but not yet converted into law firms or mortuaries. She peered in at her table at the restaurant, at the couple who had only water glasses before them as they sat scrutinizing menus. Audrey walked by. She and Audrey did not acknowledge each other's acquaintance.

She looked again at the flyers in the foyer, a feeling of panic starting to squeeze her chest. She counted to three (*one aw-loo, two aw-loo, three aw-loo*) then looked again at the couple at her table. She looked at them for five counts, and then she turned on her heel and pushed open the outer door and returned to the street.

~

49.

It was a Living Estate sale, that's what the flyer said. But the clothes arranged on the stripped double bed belonged to a dead man. Stretched v-neck sweaters, wide, striped ties, a white handkerchief still in the box. Suspenders. Scuffed oxfords, worn at the heels. Hanging in the closet were the shirts, eight or ten of them, button-down office shirts, limp, their poly-cotton blend nubbly and rough to the touch. A couple dressier shirts in dry cleaner plastic. She touched one, not knowing what else to do, feeling the eyes of the estate seller. The house smelled of cats and air freshener and something else.

She had not really intended to go to the estate sale. She had noted that it was on her block. Simply that. She had turned back from the restaurant, her table occupied, her day derailed. She had begun walking back home, an opposite course from her usual trek over the bridge, down the steel stairs, along the river path. She saw the Number Five bus pass, going down Broadway; it wouldn't come round for another forty minutes. She walked back to her home, with an afternoon ahead of her, an afternoon with nothing at the end, no small reward, no lighting of the rose lamp for several hours, and nothing new once it was lit.

When she came upon the sign that said Estate Sale she turned up the walk without counting, she just let her legs carry her, her heart beating fast.

The estate seller had no particular interest in the suspenders or the handkerchief or the shirts, nubbly or not. The estate seller smiled brightly and said, "No, not mine!" when asked, "Is this your house?" by another potential customer, a rough man looking for work tools. "Anything in the garage?" the man demanded, striding right by the silent, withered lady in the corner of the living room who sat keeping watch over a metal change tray filled with dollar bills and quarters, the nails of her left hand scratching at the card table as if keeping time.

A mother and her young son fingered the items on the dining room table. Florist vases, imprinted shot glasses, mismatched drink coasters, cracked wooden stirring spoons, a travel alarm clock from Reader's Digest, the yellowed instructions for use wrapped around it with a rubber band. The little boy wanted to buy a bolo tie that was shaped like a dolphin. The words "Sea World" were splayed along its arc. The hunched woman at the change tray held the bolo tie briefly, cupped it stiffly in the palms of both hands, then she rasped its price, fifty cents. She carefully recorded the transaction on a legal-sized sheet of paper, her eyes extra large behind thick lenses.

The little boy wanted to touch the violin that stood displayed in its stained satin case. A collection of musical instruments were in their own corner, arranged under a hand-scrawled sign, *DON'T TOUCH!* There was a violin, a guitar, and a smaller stringed instrument that looked like a version of them both. The latches of the cases were made of graying leather.

"Don't touch!" the mother said, pointing at the sign.

One aw-loo, two aw-loo . . . She stood at the closet, not knowing quite how to leave, she stood still, her hand holding a shirt cuff. She didn't know how to turn, let go, walk away from it. It was the closet that had her frozen, the room, the bare mattress, the ashtray on the night table, the crumpled Kleenex, the book of matches. (*Don't touch!*) . . . *three aw-loo, four aw-loo* . . . And that smell, sweet and tarry. It clung to the shirts, which also had a musty odor, like stale sweat, even those in the plastic. A childhood smell, not good.

Her heart punched at the wall of her chest. She closed her eyes and held her breath. The shirt should be on a circle rack at Secret Treasure, or on a carousel with other shirts at the Bargain Box, the neon lights up bright, round price tags affixed, pink, yellow, blue, lives left behind, let go, disappeared, disembodied, no one's now, just a shirt.

(*Army aw-loo*, said Eddy, flinging the matches, and the room went up in flames.)

~

50.

The train flowed through the town like a river. Ignore the train, that was their game, do not focus on the train. It flowed through the town, collecting debris in its currents. "Unhook your eyes!" that's how Eddy said it, that's what he yelled at her from behind his mask, dancing up and down, then standing rigid and staring, laughing his high-pitched laugh. He was excited, he was full of sugar, candy, that's all they'd eaten for hours.

If you kept your eyes open and fixed, things would come to you. Look! Unhook your eyes. Unhook your eyes from the pull of the train. Let the train flow slowly by, then faster and faster, each car just a blur in a steady procession that would evaporate if you kept your eyes on the other side, the emerging image, the street lamp, the beauty parlor, the forgotten light of the OPEN sign, faster and faster, there, the OPEN sign, left on.

~

51.

Eddy's skinny limbs lay flung out in the rocks by the side of the tracks like sticks and twigs, the logs of a perfect campfire that had crumpled. His Casper the Ghost mask was knocked off, and his head was thrown back, his blue eyes open. His mask looked like the man in the moon, fallen to earth, and his face was a silver caul. A thin ribbon looped from his mouth and wrapped around his neck, red and flowing.

Her eyes opened. She felt the yellow comforter, its vigilance, its full body drape. Her eyes were open, they stayed opened, her body a vessel for the eyes, holding them in place. She didn't move. She breathed in tiny sips, no movement, no movement at all.

A crash. A replication of the sound that woke her. A scurry and a thud. Overhead. Voices. Angry, one-second barks of sound from the voices. A gasp and a wail, quickly muffled. A chanting sort of menace, a litany of words, receding, receding. Gone.

She lay in bed and listened, her eyes wide from the light of the moon. She lay with the yellow comforter pulled up to her chin, comforting her but unable to make her sleep. She listened to the train. The first sense of approach, a slight seismic shift in the earth, the floorboards, the windowpane. Then the call, far away, a combination of menace and hope. *I'm coming.* The incremental expansion, the sensation, the sound, the presence of the train. The blast, then,

sharp and near. A warning, a herald, thrilling, frightening. A presence, like a parent, a large mammal, a full-grown creature, certain
of itself. A roar, like a flood, on and on, the sound, the sensation,
rhythmic, clacking, periodic thuds like rocks rolling on the bottom
of a river. A crescendo, a screech and a crash, then a pause, cessa-
tion, an empty aural space, the train departing, leaving the valley,
leaving, leaving. Gone.

A ringing silence, like a lingering smell.

A crash. From above.

She waited for the follow-up, more swearing, some pounding,
a slammed door.

Nothing.

~

52.

They had lived there with the foster mom and the foster dad, old people, ordered in their ways. At first the house seemed thrilling in its empty neatness. There were doilies on the backs of the chairs and on the long, shiny television console. There were thin, sheer curtains, and dark, heavy curtains. There was an electric organ in the corner of the living room, with a row of knobs and two sets of keys. Above it, Jesus cast his eyes to Heaven, tidy drops of blood emerging from his crown of thorns. There was a metronome on the organ, with an arm that tick-tocked when released. Music, though, was never played.

The daytime house was silent, but it was clean and they were washed, their hands and faces, washed. The dinnertime was quiet and unsmiling, but there was food and they were washed.

The nighttime house was dirty. She and Eddy were together, but the nighttime house was cold and dark and dirty. The smell was bad and the breath was dirty.

(*Army aw-loo*, Eddy said, flinging the matches, and up the curtains marched the flames.)

~

53.

She memorized entries in the dictionary. Faultless *adj*: having no fault. She waited and watched and memorized and counted.

She was terrified for Eddy.

They told her he was gone. Since Halloween night, their happy escape. Gone.

"He's gone," they said, the many different faces.

"Eddy's gone," they leaned closer, their voices louder. She searched their eyes and counted, carefully, counted to five. When she tried to speak she made no sound.

She shook herself, and it was a dream. A waking dream.

"Eddy's gone," they said. "He's gone."

It started again from the beginning.

~

54.

If you fixed your eyes, if you stared straight ahead, the image of the other side became clearer. You could see it all, almost normal.

She walked and counted the houses. Every third house, every third one. She looked. She took note. The odd signs in the front porch windows. I BRAKE FOR HIPPIES. Why? She didn't wonder. She didn't worry about the apostrophe on Albee's or Smith's or any of them. She took note, she worried, yes, she did worry, but now it was dislodged, her worry, her fixation on the apostrophe, it was loosened and floating and this was not a good thing, it did not feel like relief.

She did her laundry and bought canned goods at the Baker Street Market and walked the town. The Baker Street Market was a corner grocery store on a side street near the railroad tracks, the last of its kind. It had two keno machines near the front door where wraithlike figures sat and peered at the screens and smoked.

She received envelopes in the mail, checks that she took to the Baker Street Market, where they were turned into money. The sad man there did not speak to her. Once he had spoken to her the way the bus driver had, saying, "How ya doin'?" but now he just nodded and took her check and gave her the money. Sometimes he said, "There ya go."

She found things secreted away in her bargains or secret treasures, in the inside pockets of coats or the side zip pockets of purses. A penny, a quarter, buttons. Printed slips and stubs. She saved these in a candy dish and sometimes looked at them as she sat in her rocker. A ticket stub. LADYSMITH BLACK MAMBAZO. University Theater. 8 p.m. She pictured Ladysmith in a big car, wearing a tall hat, driving to Secret Treasure. A grocery receipt—Celestial Slpytime. 4.29. "Slpytime" bothered her. Belgioioso Parm. 5.88. Parm was not a food. *Your cashier was Chandrika.* This from a store called Publix. "Publix." That bothered her.

Once she found a RoseArt Washable Glue Stick. And another time she found a torn, folded, ivory card with green tendril designs and on the front the words *In the River Sweet*, and on the back typed sentences . . .

> . . . *as he walked he sampled it. The*
> *banjos twanging. The mournful*
>
> *mandolin and dulcimers that collapsed time and*
> *made you feel a piece of*
>
> *another dreamy world, a time of screen doors*
> *instead of central air and sitting*
>
> *in the evening without television and long hours*
> *passed in visits. A car would have*
>
> *been a wondrous thing.*

She found notes from The Day & Night Teller. Withdrawal $200.00. Ledger Bal $1128.08. Avail Bal $1128.08. All transactions are subject to proof and verification.

~

55.

She missed the surprise of not knowing which bus. She always waited for Five now. The driver might say, "There she is!" when she climbed the steps, or he might not. He knew by now that she wouldn't answer. He used to say, "There you are!" and when she didn't answer he would start humming. When Metro became SMARTbUS he asked her what she thought.

"It's like 'Smart Us,' y'know?" he said. She didn't like it. She said nothing.

Now he usually said, "There she is!" as if there were other people on the bus, which there might be or not. Or he said nothing, just wiggled his cap down squarely over his eyebrows and shifted into gear, thinking his thoughts.

Today she wore her jean jacket and a cap. The bus driver did not comment on the skateboard with wings, the picture on her cap. He had done so once, saying, "Go, Granny!" in a moment of uncharacteristic impertinence, impatience in his voice on that particular day, his hand jerky on the gear shift. As usual, the bus driver received nothing from her in return then, not even a nod.

Today the Number Five bus was not empty. A young man sat near the front, on the sideways seats behind the driver. He talked to the driver, shouting sentences into the back of the driver's neck. He coughed into his fist, a smoker's cough. He was going to a job, he said. Sunnyside School. He slapped his pant legs like he was pleased with himself. Then he looked at her. He was a big kid, and he dressed like #1B. Droopy trousers and chains. He had a sparkling stud above the cleft of his chin. He looked at her, and then he turned back toward the driver. And then he turned his body around and looked again into her corner. He looked straight at her. And then he looked straight ahead, out the opposite window, both knees jiggling. And then he looked at her again, across the span of just five seats, as this was one of the little city buses, the little neighborhood buses. He got up and slammed his body into the other sideways seat, into the space right next to the door. Then he rang the bell, and stood, and as he left he turned around.

I saw you, his eyes said. His eyes looked right at her and they looked threatening and frightened, both those things were in his eyes. *I saw you walking.*

~

56.

A uniform at her door. A man who seemed too large, in pants that seemed too tight, his gun a prominent presence in the black holster. He wheezed. His face was red and shiny. "Ma'am," he called her. "#1B," he said, indicating the number on the door across the hall. "Second floor," he said, pointing his finger toward the ceiling. "Occupants?" He was posing a question. The door stayed open, the hall smell came in. The man peered inside. I saw you, he said. I saw you walking. I saw you walking to here. Complaints. Information. Whereabouts. He held a photo in his hand, and he showed it to her. It was #1B, trapped in there, without his black hat, his shaved head making him look vacant, bare, unoccupied. His big ears, exposed. His eyes staring. Staring at her.

She had not seen #1B for several days. Not since she had come home and had to make her way through a cluster of big boys, men, on the building's walkway, gathered around a barbeque set up right there at the bottom of the steps that led to the dark hallway, now littered with a spilled bag of charcoal and bottles of lighter fluid and empty hot dog packages and beer cartons. #1B had elaborately bowed and pretended to tip a hat to her, touching his forehead and twirling his fingers down towards the ground. She had seen the other big boy, the boy on the bus going up Butler Creek, the boy whose eyes had looked at her. He hadn't seen her; he had been talking and laughing, coughing thickly at the end of his laugh, then taking a deep drag on his cigarette. She hadn't looked at the others, five or six more, all of them laughing and smoking and drinking the beer, huddled together around the barbeque, the day cold, the music from the window loud. She had scurried around the big boys and up the steps and then hesitated in the foyer, some of them watching her through the open door. She had turned her back and dipped down and brushed her hand quickly behind the radiator, finding her key, her safety.

~

She stood a long time and looked at her collection of scarves. She counted them as she stood, her body pulsing, rocking, pushed with an invisible finger, nudged in the small of her back. There were twenty scarves, exactly that. She cast her eyes over their colors and shapes. Stripes, blocks, circles, flowers. She knew which scarves were from the Bargain Box and which from Secret Treasure. She remembered the occasion of each purchase, the sky, the air, the day. She looked at the scarves and felt calmer then, briefly at ease.

She had not spoken to the man who'd seemed too large, the uniform at the door. He had looked at her and he had looked at the dim hallway, at the empty beer cartons, the spilled charcoal and bottles of lighter fluid. She shook her head and did not speak and soon he went away.

Now she looked at her scarves. She looked at their colors, arranged. Reds to blues to greens to golds. Then she turned on the rose lamp and sat in the rocker. *I saw you, I saw you.* She rocked.

~

57.

The yellow comforter was fresh and clean, it being the comforter-washing Monday of the month. She smoothed it on the end of the bed, folded back, arranged so that she could pull it up over herself when she lay flat. She had woken early and had done her washing, the washroom empty. She had done her shopping, the Baker Street Market busy in its own way, more than the usual number of vagrants smoking outside the front door, orange cellophane-wrapped popcorn balls for sale in a box next to the cash register.

Her collection of scarves were all ironed and organized on the shelf in an overlapping pattern so that an inch strip of each scarf was exposed. The key was in the china saucer, since she was home. When she was gone, it lay secret behind the radiator, waiting for her return. When she was home, it lay in the china saucer, waiting for her to go out.

The carpet was swept. She did not own a vacuum, so she swept the carpet in the small sitting room, the growing pile of dust and threads making its way gradually into the kitchen where she could more easily sweep it into the dustpan. After she swept, she brushed the carpet with her fingers, down on her knees, making sure the shag threads flowed uniformly. She felt embarrassed, ashamed, kneeling down on the floor like that, but that was the only way to get it right.

She scrubbed the kitchen sink with damp sections of the Shopper, strewn near the outer doorway of the building, free to all. The chemicals from the newsprint made the stainless steel shine. She scrubbed her toilet and sink and tub with balls of nylon netting, picked up at the Bargain Box in the For Free bin. She wore the gloves that came with her Loving Care hair dye. Sometimes the Loving Care dye was brown, sometimes it was blonde, sometimes it was ash. She found the dented packages on the makeup shelf at Secret Treasure, which also had an assortment of miniature bottles of shampoo and lotion and small paper-wrapped soaps from Coastal Hotels and Resorts.

She scrubbed her kitchen floor with suds made from adding a bit of her clothes soap to a bucket of water. Then she poured the water into her toilet bowl and swished the nylon netting around with a long-handled spoon that she kept for just that purpose under the bathroom sink.

Back in the kitchen, she stripped off the Loving Care gloves and wiped off the tin cans in her cupboard with her bare hand: three cans of mandarin orange slices, two cans of Chicken of the Sea tuna, one can of cream of mushroom soup, one can of corn. She arranged her packets of jam, brought home from the restaurant. Strawberry, grape, marmalade; red, purple, orange.

The Mondays that were grocery shopping days and also comforter-washing days were very busy. And today had been a cleaning day. She was setting things to rights.

When everything was scrubbed and brushed and wiped and it was almost time to leave, she washed her hands and face and brushed her mottled, baby-fine hair (on the blonde side today), and chose her hat. She chose her satchel. She buttoned up her coat, though the day was mild. She took her key from its saucer. She looked back at her home before opening the door. She looked at all her things, and they watched her leave.

~

58.

The little old man, the former #1B, he was gone. Dave the taxi driver, with his crooked eyeglasses, he was gone. Eddy was gone, she knew that, gone. She only had Audrey. *Audrey aw-loo.* It wasn't First Wednesday, it wasn't any Wednesday, but still she walked straight to the restaurant, no stopping. She planned to sit at her corner table and order the soup and salad combo, paying full price. She planned to eat her pasta salad in eight to ten small bites, as if things were normal. She wore her taffy-pink beret. The day was mild, though the trees of the town, blown by the wind, were bare. It was Halloween.

She stood at the restaurant door, frozen. It wasn't that her table was occupied. It sat empty there, waiting for her. A little orange plastic jack o' lantern was placed in its center, and there were more jack o' lanterns in the centers of all the tables.

It was Audrey. Audrey moved from the kitchen to the tables and back again, carrying the plates, taking orders with her order pad, all fluid, her expression calm. The other waitress and the cook wore costumes, the waitress a cat, with ears and whiskers, the cook a Q-tip, or so he kept explaining, adjusting the tall wad of cotton on his head.

Audrey wore no costume, just a wound. Her forehead was wrinkled above her brows, a constant crease, as if she were worried or trying not to cry. Under her brows, one eye was frightened and the other was bandaged, the skin surrounding it maroon and mottled. And then she was putting on her coat in the kitchen and handing her order pad to another girl and she was leaving out the back, the cook calling, "Take it easy, Audrey."

~

If you kept your eyes open and fixed, things would come to you. The houses flowed slowly by as she walked. The houses and the yards and the trees and the cars in the street. They flowed in a steady procession. She did not look ahead to the third house. She waited for it to come as she walked. Every third house moved toward her, growing larger, and, already diminishing, floated past. Sometimes she saw every third house as if she were on a river, she moved and the house stood still. At other times she stayed still and the house moved toward her, like a train car linked, inevitable, it pulled and pushed through her world, the moment, that street.

It is Monday, she thought, her legs walking, her beret snug against the breeze. Her mind clicked the words over, snapped them down. *It is Monday*, she told herself, pulling on her acrylic gloves without breaking her pace, tucking her satchel under her arm. *It is Monday afternoon.* She could smell the Macy's perfume absorbed by the gloves, Liaison, Tanzibar, and BEAUTY. *It is Monday afternoon for everyone, all across the town.*

~

VI.

THE TREE

59.

She lay in bed, planning her day. Mondays usually were hectic. "You seem sort of heckity," Dirk might say at breakfast, as she packed her yoga bag and looked for the checkbook and brushed Clark's teeth, his little pointy head in a football hold. She did this once a week to improve his breath and keep him young longer. She could have chosen some other day, but she did it on Mondays because that was her "Better Bliss" yoga day, a special class. She used one activity to cue another, a handy reminder tool.

This Monday, though, she was going to break the mold. It was Halloween, she was skipping yoga. She already had their candy, stuff they all liked, Snickers and gummi bears and malted milk balls, all piled up in the black plastic cauldron. She wanted to make some chili. That was the tradition. Chili at their house, then the kids would go out. In the toddler years they were followed by parents sneaking whiskey into travel mugs, in the pre-teen years Alex rode herd, and last year Sammy and Walt went out alone, embarrassed to be dressing up, but reluctant to let go of it. They went out in a disconcerted state, hybrid Halloweeners, part child, part roving gang member, at least that's what you might think, given Sammy's new height and both their costumes. Skulls painted on their cheeks and chains hanging everywhere. Studded dog collars. They said some people wouldn't open their doors to them, and she could see why.

This year, trick-or-treating was proclaimed to be gay. She felt sad that it was. She had put the decorations out, but only Clark seemed to be excited by them, the little ghosts, hanging by their necks. She had always liked Halloween as a kid. Leaving the bright and busy house, into the dusk, the rattling leaves, the breeze. Escaping homework, bedtime postponed, rules suspended, even with a parent or sitter trailing behind. Becoming someone else, briefly, a princess (pink dress, pink accessories, all of it bought at Kmart), a riverboat gambler (her brother's Easter suit and a top hat with the ace of spades tucked in the band). Now she got stuck answering the door, Dirk watching TV. But she liked that too. Halloween was a doorstep holiday, not a dining room holiday, chili notwithstanding. It was out in the streets, in the public domain. The public was responsible for the success of Halloween. She was off the hook.

She did not have to feel sad about Walt. At Christmas, Thanksgiving, Easter, she felt sad when Walt hung around their house, looking at the big turkey thawing in the sink, looking at the Christmas tree at Christmas time, all the presents piled up, touching the dyed Easter eggs (Sammy specifying which ones he could touch and which ones he could not). Then the day before whichever holiday was being celebrated, Walt disappeared, taking his cue, he got lost. He was back the day after, looking at Sammy's presents, his Easter basket, saying "awesome" or "sweet," but not touching unless invited to do so.

On the days leading up to Halloween, though, Walt typically was around the house more and more, as he and Sammy planned their costumes. And on Halloween night, he was right there, front and center. There was no accompanying parent hovering, never had been a parent following Walt around on Halloween. Overtly, Sammy envied Walt's parentless state. But she noticed that Sammy could be solicitous of Walt, too, such as when he offered Walt her padded bra once to use for Mickey Mouse ears, necessitating that she make Walt some ears herself, out of cardboard, muttering under her breath about Walt's damn deadbeat so-called Mom.

This year she could hear Sammy on the phone to Walt saying, "Nah." Just that. No Halloween.

~

60.

Once the chili was served, she would put on her mom-at-the-door costume, her biker chick costume (wash-off tattoos and a leather vest), or her schoolmarm costume (black glasses and bun wig, with fake frowning eyebrows), or, the one time, her Monica Lewinsky costume (a big beret and kneepads). Monica was a mistake. She had to tell Sammy she was a funny French hockey lady, and he was puzzled, and she felt ashamed. Still, it was good, it was all good. You could be anyone at Halloween.

But she probably wouldn't dress up this year, since Halloween was gay. Plus, she needed to get things ready for the cleaning gal. First time coming. She had to dig out a few rat's nests, though she wasn't going to get fussed up about it. Her mood watch from SkyMall had changed from gray (anxious) to blue (calm). The heat sensitive dial changed color with the body's temperature. It was sort of a joke, but she liked to consult it. Her temperature, hence mood, apparently, was calm. She knew if she went to yoga her calmness would be endangered by the substitute instructor, who encouraged everyone to ask their various body parts what they wanted to do. This she found annoying. She did not want to ask her knee if it wanted to go further. She did not want to ask her back to arch. She didn't want to be in charge of her body. Her body was too much.

She lay in bed with the newspaper and her notepad and a cup of coffee. She wrote:

Costume. Donald Rumsfeld? (Dirk's suit, retro glasses)

Then she crossed that out and wrote:

Chili—Just do it!

Dirk stood in the doorway, disconcerted. Lying in bed at odd hours was his thing. Clark stood poised at Dirk's feet, his eyes glistening, waiting for the slightest reason to bark.

"You do it." She said about Clark. "I'm tired of his teeth."

Clark's dental hygiene was going the way of Sammy's good attitude. She couldn't manage everything. Dirk had put a Parenting Coach flyer on the refrigerator, right next to the Go Fetch number, as if that were taking action. He said he liked the idea of a coach better than a counselor. A half-hour session of parenting coaching cost $70 and was done over the phone.

~

61.

She said to Dirk: "I'm glad Sammy has a friend." And then they both frowned, watching Sammy bob down the walk looking up at the twig guy, the guy with the wide-legged pants. He bobbed too, and Sammy, it was obvious, was copying this weird, dipping gait, as if there were low-hanging branches they both were trying to avoid. The twig guy, with his shaved head. No big deal, her and Dirk's accountant had a shaved head. But that zigzag tattoo on the back of his skull, sort of like a lightning bolt, a cartoon thought. Well, probably their accountant would get one of those next.

Sammy was jabbering, his hands in his pockets. He'd been unusually perky since he woke up, happy, she guessed, since it was a school PIR day, but maybe, she sort of hoped, because it was Halloween. He was snappish, too, though that was nothing new these days. He told Clark to shut the fudge up, though he didn't say "fudge."

She had no idea what a PIR day was, she just knew that it meant a random day off from school for Sammy, who typically slept all morning instead of bouncing around the house. Now he was dipping and jabbering and looking up at the twig guy's face, which was fixed in a smile.

"It," she said to Dirk, as they both looked out the living room window at the two receding backs.

"What?" said Dirk.

"It," she repeated, looking around the room distractedly. She had the feather duster in her hand. She was dusting the books, in anticipation of the cleaning gal.

"That book, the Stephen King book, the one called *It*. That guy reminds me of the clown."

~

62.

Walt was a source of information, a source of jokes, a source of trouble. But Walt was small, unlike the twig guy. Walt was Sammy's age, and smaller than Sammy, smaller than most kids at that grade level. Probably from poor nutrition and from eating rocks on the school bus and other risky behaviors. Walt was trouble, no question. But he also had a gappy grin that he couldn't help grinning. It wasn't uniform, it wasn't fixed, it was all over the place. Walt's feelings were splayed upon his face.

She remembered driving Sammy and Walt to their first middle school dance, in sixth grade, just the year previous, when they were twelve. Sammy had been occupied with how many quarters he had in his pocket, thinking ahead to the pop machine. But Walt was thinking about the dance. "Are you scared?" she heard him ask Sammy under his breath. It was an honest question, not intended for her ears, not purposefully fashioned to make Walt seem endearing. Despite Walt's wild grin, he had a lot of purposeful adult-directed behaviors, such as shaking hands and calling mothers "ma'am," a habit Sammy found outrageous. These were coping behaviors, Sara Greeley-Greenough said. They were strategies. They were like the elaborate courtliness of a panhandler. Walt's upbringing had been sketchy (Sara used a word she'd picked up from Seth), so Walt had learned coping behaviors to garner acceptance.

But this hadn't been that. The question "Are you scared?" was posed in a quiet voice, an undertone, almost a whisper.

~

63.

She would come home from yoga class or Pilates class or the health club and the house would smell like dinner. That was the idea. But she was skipping yoga today, too damn bad. (That substitute instructor's pants fit funny.) She was creating and retaining her own sense of calm, her quiet space, an autonomous bliss. She was going to make the chili.

She had planned to empty her brain, then soften it, but now the house was filling up with people, people who were her family. So ok, she would do the pre-cleaning and a little pre-planning. It was good to recognize options and honor ambivalence in middle age. She wanted to explain the Crock-Pot. This wasn't going to be a cleaning gal situation, it was going to be a housekeeper situation, one step up. No way was she going to have the housekeeper thinking they were hopeless slobs.

Sammy went off with the twig guy, Mr. Pick Up Stix, God knows, but Dirk hung around, watching her dust the living room. He said he didn't feel well, but she thought he was avoiding his work life. He said there'd been inter-office strife.

"You mean 'intra-office'," she said, "you only have the one office, so there's no 'inter' to it." No, he said, she was wrong. He rubbed his stomach and gazed at the ceiling, his legs on the coffee table. It was *inter*-office because it was an internal matter. *Inter*nal.

Clark was throwing himself against his doggy gate in the kitchen, rhythmically, like a long-term inmate. The gate was a sporadic thing, one or the other of them would stick him in the kitchen with his chew toys and wedge the gate in the doorway, just to get him out from underfoot. He'd immediately begin the full-body throw, as nerve-jarring as his actual presence. The shudder of the doggy gate made him sound much larger than he actually was, which was about the size of a deformed cat. He was a cat-rat cross, and she couldn't fathom why they'd ever got him.

She dusted, her eye on the little plaid bag, just where she had seen it and put it on her To Think About list and then transferred to her Sometime Soon list. It was next to *It*. And it was next to *French Women Don't Get Fat*, which she happened to know was wrong, because they do. They get fat, or they become a bag of bones. They age, sicken, and die. Like everybody else.

Next on the shelf was a hollow *Encyclopedia Yearbook* for the year 2000, the New Millennium, a fake book that was supposed to be a place for stashing stuff, legal documents, extra cash, maybe a tiny hand gun. Maybe your cyanide pills, if the New Millennium didn't look too promising. Sammy had stuffed it with Legos, an eight-year-old's important items, though already on the wane for him back then at the turn of the century. She opened it and looked inside, Dirk preoccupied with programming his cellphone alarm to ring in five minutes and make him get off the couch. The Legos were still there, some of them still holding the shape of half-fashioned dinosaurs. Sammy used to make dioramas inside packing boxes, predators stalking prey, she'd have to go look, he'd always insist. He would set it up in the living room and she would have to dust around it for several weeks and they would all yell at Clark to stay away.

She carefully put the fake book back, first arranging the Legos so that the book would close up tight and keep the Legos in place, a secret cache from the past. She wanted to refer to *It*, see if she was right about the twig guy and the clown. The clown kept popping up here and there, that much she remembered. The clown looked sweet and silly but was not. The clown kept smiling, a uniform half-moon. You didn't want to know what the clown was smiling about.

~

64.

Sammy's Halloween costumes when he was real little had been skeletons. Bones painted onto black t-shirts in fluorescent silver, or once, in preschool, an actual rattling cage of plastic bones encasing his tiny torso. Sunnyside honored the dark side, the children learned to say death in Spanish, "Muerte!" the Minnows crowed. They had their costume parade out in the schoolyard the day after Halloween, on the Day of the Dead. They were allowed to say "dead" in English, too.

At Butler School that all had been deemed inappropriate. Morbid. It might remind the children of something bad. Such as mortality. It was to safeguard the children's safety, the principal wrote in a confused memo. As if to speak aloud the word "dead" might cause the children to die. Well, there'd been the school shootings and so forth. Columbine. Death just made the administration skittish.

So in fourth and fifth grades Sammy had been a clown for Halloween. The fourth-grade clown had been sweet and silly, flopping around in Dirk's big shoes, wearing her hair extension (a horrifying, one-time, 80's thing). The fifth-grade clown was malevolent and glaring, Sammy wearing fangs with his pancake makeup and big bucked teeth, sucking in saliva with every breath. Last year, the hybrid year, he had been a vague gang guy, the costume no longer disguise or transformation, just attitude and stance. Now it had all turned gay.

She didn't want to move the little plaid bag, expose it. Not until Dirk was gone. She wanted to process its contents by herself.

"Goodbye," she said to Dirk, thinking this might dislodge him from his chair. He picked up an issue of *Globe and Cosmos* and read aloud the cover, stalling.

"The Big Thaw: Ice on the Run, Seas on the Rise."

"Later," she said brightly, dusting all around him until his cell phone played harp music and he tossed the magazine onto the coffee table and heaved himself to his feet with a sigh and ambled out to the driveway, where he sat in the Bronco awhile, just sat there, staring. Finally she heard him drive away.

She looked at the plaid bag. She eased it out of its spot. If it was pharmaceuticals she knew where she could look things up online. Match the shape of the little pills to the substance. She'd done that once with a pill she'd found on the bathroom floor, which had turned out to be Viagra. She'd been meaning to talk to Dirk about that, she had put it on the Items for Discussion list. But whenever she got to that item she just felt sad. Or some other disaster popped up.

Faultless *adj*: having no fault. Without blemish, imperfection, or error; perfect.

She stared at the little slip of paper, about the size of a Chinese cookie fortune, but torn off, like it was for drawing straws, the letters written in careful cursive. She looked again into the bag, checked the inner zipper pocket, nothing. No pills, no pot, no stash of cash. Just the word and its definition, the handwriting unfamiliar and childish, the t's looped like ribbons on a present.

~

65.

Clark was lost. Usually he yapped like a crazed hyena when the doorbell rang, but today the chime was met with silence. How or when he'd made his escape, she had no idea. She had been distracted with the house gal, showing her the dead flies in the wall sconces. She did know that if Clark ever realized that no responsible person was in his immediate vicinity in the great outdoors, watching him do his doo-doo, then he'd take off like a bullet, in any random direction. Maybe his arthritis was a sham and he could hold his own in the Go Fetch crowd, what did she know?

Anyway, he'd somehow gotten out, and somehow fired himself off, obviously, and she'd have to wait for the cleaning gal/house-keeper, the house gal, to get a little more established and onto her tasks before there would be any time to go looking for him in the car. She wanted to find him before the trick-or-treaters started coming; he'd go cuckoo seeing them flapping down the walks. It seemed the trick-or-treaters came earlier and earlier each year, probably due to parental fears of the dark, the potential for accidents, all the stuff on the news, those kids who were allowed to commune with the dusk so swathed in reflector tape that every costume looked like a mummy no matter what.

The house gal looked a little worse for wear. She was fairly young and pretty in a drab way, but she had a patch on one eye and the skin was quite bruised. It was distasteful to look at. "Eye surgery," she said. "Will take two weeks to heal."

Sammy was upstairs in his bedroom jumping on his skateboard. Bam! Pause. Bam! Pause. He had returned alone from his walk with the twig guy, just as the house gal tutorial was reaching its main thrust (the pretty crucial explanation about not running the clothes washer and dishwasher at the same time to avoid scalding to death anyone in the shower) and he had looked at her, his loving mother, and said, "Why are *you* here?" Like he'd been planning to rendezvous with the house gal, who she didn't introduce because she'd already forgotten her name for the time being. Oh yeah, Audrey, her name was Audrey, which rang bells from yesteryear somehow; it was a name from an old-fashioned sitcom, the pal housewife next door.

She's a little old for you, Samster, wouldn't you say? She'd wanted to retort. But didn't. Retorts weren't a good idea when questions weren't questions, but, instead, random accusations. And she'd also learned from the parenting counselor not to call Sammy "Samster" if he indicated he did not like it (which he had indicated, saying it sounded like "hamster") and not to make jokes about Sammy's budding sexuality, or even say things like that, things like "budding," which could only be said with a laugh. "Emerging sexuality" was the proper term, as if Sammy's sexuality were a little groundhog peeping out, checking the weather, seeing if the coast was clear.

~

66.

She left to go look for Clark in the car. It had been hard to get dislodged. She'd wrapped up the housecleaning spiel and left the house gal limply rubbing at the stainless steel in the kitchen with a damp newspaper (a tip from *Get Simple*), and then she'd gone upstairs and performed a little token nagging about homework that concluded with her and Sammy in a mutual wrestling grip with the damn skateboard, she trying to take it away, remove it from the room, he trying to keep it at least in close proximity while he did his supposed, goddamn, fudging homework, something she had demanded happen before the chili-and-trick-or-treating, even though he said he hated chili and wasn't going out door-to-door like a douchebag. If Clark had been anywhere nearby it would have been Ground Zero. Then just as she gave up and slammed the door to Sammy's room and descended the stairs, banging her body a little against the railing on purpose to express her view toward Sammy's stance, the doorbell chimed.

It chimed mellifluously. A little buzzing bleat outside and then the deep, sonorous chord, like some kind of wacko church. Dirk's idea. He'd loaded up on items for the home one day at Home Depot, the brass dachshund, the chiming bell, some plants for the porch, potted whatnots. He said they made him feel better, at least momentarily.

She grabbed the phone, her old MO, not for safety—the house was overflowing with protection—but to get rid of the damn person, whoever the damn person might turn out to be. Such as, oh, why not, a funny little lady in a pink hat selling something, gathering signatures, a church lady, Save the Whales, who knew? She said, "Um-hum, um-hum, um-hum" into her phone, scanning the lady distractedly, as if looking for a clipboard, the place to sign, then, "Yes?" she said to the funny little lady in the taffy-colored tam o' shanter who said in a soft, cracking voice, "Well, I'll be."

"Um –hum, um-hum, uh-uh," she said to her phone, waving the hovering house gal into the living room, jingling her car keys for good measure, then, "What?" to the lady, who repeated herself, mumbling and clearing her throat.

"The Albee."

"Hang on a sec," she said to her phone, switching it to the other ear for effect, pointing the house gal toward the Pledge, then, "Who?" she said to the hat lady. (Familiar, the shade of that tam, it was exactly like Ellen's pink-wear, all that damn stuff she'd dumped off at Secret Treasure, the Breast Cancer Awareness pink-wear that she really didn't want, being plenty damn aware, thank you.)

But the little lady was already on her way back down the walk, stepping carefully around the lumber for Sammy's vert ramp-in-progress, a sloping ramp that was designed to get a skateboarder airborne, but that, in their front yard, never seemed to achieve full construction.

The twig guy, ambling back up the street, elaborately tipped a pretend hat at the little lady, as she scurried down the walk. Her twigs were fine, *fine* she assured the guy again as he came up the walk. He was both smelly and creepy, she decided, his smile like a ribbon sewn onto his face, his ears sticking out like a cartoon, not funny. Sammy came thumping down the stairs and out the door, giving a high five to the twig guy, just to get her goat, she knew, before slapping his skateboard down and sailing away down the street, narrowly missing the pink-hatted bag lady. The twig guy shambled off, toodle-oo.

Not even yet time for trick-or-treat and their neighborhood was full of loonies.

~

67.

Women, as women, it seems they are
always trying to be
                                 sympathetic: STOP. It may get
you raped, or killed. Ted Bundy,
        the serial
        killer, was a good-looking, personable man,
who ALWAYS played
        on the sympathies of unsuspecting women, he
walked with a cane, or a limp . . .
        (Etc. etc.) Love, Pa.

~

They found Clark just before chili time. She'd noticed that his
leash was missing, so she figured maybe Sammy had forgotten to take
it off him after their recent, unprecedented trot. Sometimes Clark
had a leash dangling from his collar all the livelong day. The little
sweater was there, hanging on its hook. But no leash. And no Clark.

So after touring the neighborhood in the car she did a systematic search of the bushes around the house. He might have gotten
hung up while doing his business or looking for his cell phone.
Then she did a systematic search inside the house, her heart starting

to constrict in a weird way. The house was empty of people by then. Dirk still at work, Sammy off again, shirking his studies, whizzing into the late afternoon shadows on his skateboard like he was fleeing something. Everyone hither and thither and yon. The house gal, not exactly a marvel of efficiency, finally finishing and accepting her check and heading down the street for the bus, her shoulders hunched like it was cold, which it wasn't.

Clark was thirteen. In doggy years that was 91. Oh my god, he was a nanogenerian or whatever. No wonder he acted so bonkers.

She looked in all the rooms, realizing, by the time she got to the basement laundry area, that she was thinking about crying. No Clark. Such silence. They'd bought Clark when Sammy was a baby, just walking. Sammy and this new puppy from Petland had taken turns being on different sides of the doggy gate, which had also been a baby gate. They had mostly bonded through plastic triangles, since Clark's puppy nails were sharp and Sammy would put absolutely anything into his mouth at that time, including puppy accidents. But they had bonded. They had overcome the obstacles.

Back upstairs she stood in the living room, which smelled like Pledge but looked just the same as it always did, and she listened to the ticking clock, gasping a little when it wound up to toll the hour, the chime melding with her exasperated hiccup of grief. Then she sat down in the hunting hound chair, her head on her knees and her arms hanging to the floor, a modified yoga pose, the child's pose, her favorite.

"Well, for crying out loud!"

Dirk. She darted to the window and saw him out there in the yard gazing up into the weeping birch. She looked up. There was Clark, barely discernible in the gloom, hanging, his little legs clustered together like barbequed chicken wings, his round eyes flashing a bit in the glow of the setting sun, fixed and staring.

~

68.

A woman hears a crying baby on her porch late at night. On *America's Most Wanted*. (Her father called to ask if she was watching.) A woman is home alone and she hears a crying baby outside, and so she calls the police because she thinks this is weird. The police tell her, "Whatever you do, DO NOT open the door . . ." The woman listens some more, thinking maybe she was wrong, maybe it was a cat. No, it is a crying baby, she is sure of it, and it sounds like the baby has crawled near a window, and she is worried that it will crawl to the street and get run over. The police say, "We already have a unit on the way, whatever you do DO NOT open the door." The police say that they think a serial killer has a baby's cry recorded and is using it to coax women out of their homes thinking someone dropped off a baby. They say they have not verified it, but have had several calls by women saying that they hear babies crying outside their doors when they're home alone at night.

~

69.

That smell, the same funny smell. It's what she remembered from the little lady at the door, the hat lady, when she thought about her, way later. When she tried to ID the perpetrator, the robber and/or brutalizer of innocent victims. The list of possible perps was short. There was the twig guy, a likely suspect, but she didn't want to be prejudiced against the youth culture. Maybe he was just one of those twenty-somethings with the pants. So why did the police have his photo? He looked at her out of the photo with an unfocused gaze, cog-in-the-machine, pawn of the system, destiny's foot soldier, a mechanical look, somewhat like the robot bravado Alex had attempted, unsuccessfully, in his big 8x10 military photo, the one displayed at his funeral, his face dominated by the giant hat. The eyes trying, trying to be vacant.

Then there was the cleaning gal, but she was such a dishrag, a sad sack, with her battered eye, likely story; she didn't look like she could afford eye surgery, she looked battered, plain and simple. It was hard to imagine her perpetrating anything. And she hadn't done any cleaning in the football field-sized bedroom, her and Dirk's, where the family jewels went missing, so to speak. Ugly, super-expensive jewels, all Dirk's mom's. She'd bequeathed the jewels (some swirly opal and diamond creations and a honking-big raw emerald ring, and a long string of honest-to-god pearls) soon after their wedding, saying they could pawn them if need be, not having much faith at that time in Dirk's earning potential.

There wasn't Sammy, Sammy wasn't part of the line-up, Sammy was only thirteen, not to mention being somewhat related. Sammy hadn't rummaged in her drawers since he'd fished out the padded bra for mouse ears, many a Halloween ago. Sammy now had a horror of her drawers, also the conjugal bedroom. He'd put an invisible force field around the parental spaces and stayed away.

Sammy in cahoots with the twig guy? No. No way. Sammy said he thought the twig guy was cool, his shaved head and all, the zigzag tattoo, but then he thought a lot of people were cool, people you wouldn't exactly want to have to dinner.

Sammy wasn't in cahoots with the twig guy, she told the police, he had only gone off with him for a bit, down the block, to show him Seth Greeley-Greenough's graffiti art, which was spray-painted in dayglo colors all over one outside wall of the Greeley-Greenough's garage, a raised fist and lots of swirls and something that looked suspiciously like a penis but Sara Greeley-Greenough said it was the stem of a frangipani flower, which had to do with an Eastern religion. This all was on the wall between the garage and the house and you couldn't really see it from the street unless you really looked.

The twig guy had asked about this artwork and Sammy had explained it, acting as a little neighborhood docent, since Seth was gone.

The police were just going through the motions. This was petty stuff, there'd been a rash of it, laptops lifted off of car seats, small appliances taken from homes, maybe some silver, people leaving doors unlocked had to realize the risk.

But it puzzled her, and disturbed her, the jewels missing from her sock drawer. They'd been inside some argyle socks she never wore, a tip from *Get Simple*. Forget buying a home safe, just hide your valuables in ordinary places, where burglars wouldn't think to look. She knew right away they were missing because this is where she kept her Lorazepam, too, which also was missing. She'd thought she might take half a Lorazepam, after the events of the day, so she went up to her sock drawer, looking for the argyle stash. The tip was in a special Risk Management issue, the one that advocated freezing your nonessential credit cards in ice in a Tupperware Freeze-It, or maybe that was the Disappear Your Debt issue, the credit card being frozen to make it harder to use. They had adopted that practice, or tried to, but Dirk blew up the microwave trying to thaw the ice to get at the card, which apparently had some metal components; maybe they all do, maybe in the hologram.

"The missing jewels," the police said, "let's get back to that."

The missing jewels. It sounded so funny, like a game of Clue. But it felt creepy. Somebody had been in their house. In their bedroom. In her drawers.

There was that odd little hat lady, out of the blue. And that smell, recurring.

The little lady hadn't even stepped into the foyer, and she had retreated quickly. But did she circle on back? Did she have an accomplice? Things had been weird around the house for some weeks, cash disappearing, stuff going missing. It was a stressful time, nothing was quite right. In the whole damn world. Shock and awe, and all that hoohaw. Weird things happening in the town, too. Someone had taken a pot shot at the WIM women, for example. Sara was full of the story, how the shot had zinged past her ear. It was determined to have been a BB from a BB gun, but still, BB's could do damage, and that BB had dinged Sara's earring. Creepy-weird!

Note → If the predator has a gun and you are not under his Control

ALWAYS RUN! The predator

will only hit you (a running target) 4 in 100
times; and even then, it most likely WILL NOT
be a vital
organ.
RUN, Preferbly in a zig-zag pattern! (Love, Pa)

The little lady hadn't looked like she was prepared to shoot 100
times. Was she some kind of walking wounded, herself, a bag lady,
destitute? What was she doing in the Butler Creek area? Was she a
local terrorist of some sort, done up to look harmless, looking for a
safe haven? But maybe she was just collecting signatures for a cause,
or maybe it was a Halloween thing, or an anti-Halloween thing, a
church something or other?

But that smell, that funny smell. No, not funny, not funny at all.
Expensive, that was the smell. Maybe you could call that funny. It was
Liaison, which was something like $86 for a little 4-ounce vial. Sort
of understated and musky, she finally pegged it. Not exactly the scent
du jour of a funny, mousey-haired little lady with schizo eyes.

She couldn't see spending that kind of money for perfume. So
when she smelled it around the house, she thought it was funny, that
is, odd. And it seemed funny-odd to her now that she hadn't iden-
tified it, wafting around their house, their house with its familial
tensions and spit-soaked doggy toys, that she hadn't once thought
of the smell as perfume, a woman's perfume, belonging to a woman
not-her. Someone had been in their house. Someone had riffled
through her drawers. Sammy was too little for women. Dirk? Dirk
was too tired. A perpetrator, an invader of some sort. She herself
wore SPORTY body splash, if she wore anything at all. Anything
in the way of scent. Of course she wore other things, lots of things,
in terms of clothes. Layers and layers of things. Twenty-four seven.

~

70.

Coach Murphy was not as strong as he looked. His long legs were shaking a bit as they all looked up at him. She, Dirk, and Sammy, returned, and then Sara Greeley-Greenough, who came down the street when she saw them gathered in a semi-circle under a tree, maybe thinking this was some kind of communal Druid thing for Halloween, a shared neighborhood holiday activity. Now Sara held their black cauldron of candy out to the sporadic clusters of costumed kids, who, walking backwards, distractedly fished out a treat while following everyone's gaze up the tree. They were curious, but on the trick-or-treat clock.

Coach Murphy had to first go back to his garage and get some clippers. It seemed a little dicey, climbing up through the weeping birch branches carrying the clippers, which was why she hadn't let Dirk do it. Dirk had already fallen out of one tree during their married life, early on, when he thought he might do some pruning.

"Murph's feeling a little compromised because of his chemo," said Sara. Dirk stood up straight at these words, a gesture that looked like affront, but was really surprise. He cast his gaze at the horizon, the end of the block, and then he quickly paced around in place, his arms folded, he paced a small circle. Then he looked at his family members with an expression intended to be blank and baffled, an expression that succeeded. She returned the look, averting her face so Sara wouldn't see.

"Well, it'll do that to a guy," Dirk finally said.

Sammy's eyes were wet and wide, fixed on Clark.

"He's dead," he said, the words constricted, the tone pre-teen. He had both hands in his hair, grasping it like it was hay, pressing his clenched fists on his scalp like his brains were escaping.

Clark was hanging motionless from his collar about twenty or thirty or forty feet up in the tree. She could never estimate feet. A driveway's length up the tree. She tried to form an image of Clark climbing the tree and couldn't. Clark could do some unlikely things. He could do a near-perfect back flip. He could get toast off the table. He could use a cell phone. There had been a few calls made on the lost cell phone, they showed up on the bill. She figured if he jabbed at it enough, and gnawed on it enough, numbers could become punched that would result in a call. She figured he had it stashed somewhere out in the bushes. They were all supposed to wait for him to do his doo-doo and then bring him right back in the house, but they didn't always. It was a hassle. A hassle that a fence might help. But, it was true, Clark could weasel his way in or out of anywhere. Anyway, they'd never know, would they, because the fence Dirk had started stayed incomplete, just one section of rustic ranch-style split posts that had cost a fortune and was full of slivers.

Once they even forgot Clark outside overnight. He'd done his runaway thing, his "I'm a rocket" thing, and then they'd all become sidetracked and in the morning they had found him shivering on the back porch, too cold to even bark, because they'd also forgotten to put on his little sweater. Whoops.

But she couldn't picture Clark climbing that tree. His legs were too short and they didn't really bend much, his little drumstick legs. She supposed if he were in some kind of lathered up fury he could propel himself up the tree before his little legs even knew what was happening. He could launch himself despite himself, if he were really provoked or freaked, if he were chasing a chipmunk or trying to escape from something, a bigger dog maybe, or Sara's lesbian cat. But he was way out on a limb and way up that tree. He was hung up by his collar and his leash was wrapped around his neck a bunch of times, his neck and all down his little Smokey Joe body. Sammy used to say he looked like a Smokey Joe, one of those little pre-cooked weenies. She was crying some, remembering this, crying in little hiccups, trying to mask it.

Weeping birches didn't usually get so tall unless they were pretty old, in which case—she'd been told by a legitimate tree service guy—they were probably inwardly decrepit and ready to crash down at any minute. She'd been expecting that to happen any day. They'd come home and the weeping birch would have prostrated itself upon the house and yard. She knew that's how it would likely go. She'd been expecting that. But she hadn't expected this.

Clark looked like he had been flung. She didn't want to admit it, but she had to admit it. He looked very much as if he had been thrown into the tree. Tossed up to his death—a de facto gallows. He twisted a bit in the breeze, and she could see his sharp nails shining.

When Coach Murphy brought Clark's stiff little body out of the tree, his pant legs riding up his veined legs as he slid down the last section, juggling the dog and the clippers and looking for a foot hold, she held her breath, hoping to hear the snuffling gagging noise that Clark made when he was overwhelmingly excited.

Maybe he wasn't dead at all, just petrified. Or thrilled. Sometimes it was hard to tell with Clark. Sometimes when he got carried away with his household dramas, his barking at the doorbell and at the oven timer and the clothes dryer, or with his social encounters, his trembling, unprovoked antagonisms toward leaves and squirrels and Sara's cat Simone, he became worked up in an almost embarrassing way, even though they'd had him fixed.

But he lay in Sammy's arms now like a found object, stuffed animal, just a pretend dog, gazing up into Sammy's weeping face with button eyes, and the snuffling gagging noise was absent; there was not even a whimper, there was just absence, a total absence, a blank emptiness in the place where Clark used to be.

~

71.

Coach Murphy had been in the service, but he had not been in Vietnam. He had been given a medical discharge during training, for reasons that were vague. Something about a chemical warfare practice maneuver that had gone awry. He didn't really like to tell this story, but Sara Greeley-Greenough got it out of him when she was doing an oral history.

Peter Greenough did not go to Vietnam. His draft number was called, but on the advice of a doctor who also was his uncle, he ran 15 miles to his physical exam and got off on account of high blood pressure.

Dirk had been assigned a lottery number in the last year of Vietnam. He still remembered it: 311. That was the name of a rock band—metal band or a punk band or emo band, she couldn't keep them straight. Sammy volunteered this band information when Dirk told the fairly short story about his draft number yet again at a Family Meal with "Military Service" as its topic. The information that 311 was the name of a band was a new twist to an otherwise standard family story, which went like this—Dirk: "I still remember my lottery number." Them: "What was it?" (They might say this, or they might just go, "Um.") Dirk: "311." And that was the end of the story.

Only when Sara Greeley-Greenough got Dirk to expand on the topic did she herself realize that he brought up his lottery num-

ber all the time, especially after Alex, not because he wanted to
claim some Vietnam glory, some "I ain't no Senator's son" latter-day
cachet. After Alex, when Sara G-G sat there at the kitchen counter
bar with her oral history notebook, peering intently at Dirk and
talking about the capriciousness of fate, Dirk just nodded. When
Sara brought in indigenous religions, something she was prone to
do at the drop of a hat, and spoke of a benevolent/malevolent faceless
god, or rather goddess, he looked totally confused. But when she
said, "311. Wow, you were really lucky," Dirk bent over, almost in
the yoga pose, the child's pose, he bent over with his elbows on his
knees and his face in his hands. Then after a while he said, "Yup."

Both she and Dirk perked up when Sammy volunteered the info
about Dirk's lottery number being the name of a band. Sammy had
been in a band, briefly. She and Dirk were never sure what his role
was, since he didn't play any musical instruments or really sing. The
band had disbanded soon after it was formed, for artistic reasons.
They had played at a middle school ice cream social in the courtyard
and had been accused by their peers (whose criticism of their form
really was meant to express disdain for the format) of being too
"emo," which didn't exactly mean emotional, maybe the opposite.
They didn't scream enough with rage, like Korn. Those Korn posters, the puppets with their mouths sewn shut, they were misleading.
Korn screamed like hell. Maybe Sammy's role had been Screamer,
and he had failed. They'd never know.

Sammy's band never had settled on a name, but there had been
possibilities, one-word or hyphenated slashes of attitude. Volt.
Krud. *Crank. Krunk. Ker-sputum. Clump.* When Sammy told her about
the "too emo" complaint and hinted that he might have held some
responsibility for the band's failure, that he'd been afraid to exhibit
raw fury, she made a joke. She said they should've called the band
"Eco-Emu-Emo." This kind of thing just popped out of her mouth

and then it was too late. Sammy never mentioned the band again, or any band at all, not to them, not until he volunteered this information at The Family Meal about there being a group in existence called 311. They were glad he was sharing, but she suspected that he said this, volunteered the information, as a way of shirking the scheduled discussion, which was going to be about—1. Responsibilities, and 2. Options—in the wake of Alex.

Sammy never mentioned Alex now. He didn't even want to hear the name "Alex." There had been a buy-a-brick fundraising campaign for the new addition at Sunnyside, and, despite Dirk's rants and petitions about the expansion, and despite Sammy's total avoidance of the topic of Alex, she had bought a brick for him, for Alex. It was engraved with Alex's name and dates, Sammy's name beneath.

~

Alex's father, Dwayne, had not been in Vietnam. He'd had a student deferment and went to the university and then various other colleges for eight years, eventually becoming Director of Advancement and Careers at his matriculating school, where he never missed a home game, Go Pioneers.

~

72.

Alex, in his last year of high school, shaved his head to show his allegiance to his mother, but then it had to be shaved all over again when he enlisted, effectively wiping out the allegiance and replacing it with regulation. He looked like a torture victim in his photos on MySpace that Sammy showed her, a hostage, or an inmate of a concentration camp, somehow the raw skin on his head made his eyes look black and blue. The big hat in the official military photo made him look a little better, at least not sick, even if ludicrous. When she said Alex looked ludicrous in that big hat, Sammy said that was the name of a music guy. Ludacris.

Sammy shaved his own head to show his allegiance to Alex, when the news came, and at Alex's funeral and burial he shivered uncontrollably, as if his thick, straight, strawlike hair had been his primary source of warmth during all of his short years. At the after-party, the Celebration of Life, Celeste stood up at the microphone and referred to Sammy and Ellen as "my beloved skinheads." She smiled broadly and bravely, setting an example. Ellen usually kept her bald chemo-head covered up with a soft beret or a marginally okay wig. But now Ellen was defiant. That's what Celeste said, beaming at everyone from the podium. Celeste was improvising, trying to give the crowd a heads-up that they were not to let grief ruin the party. She saluted Ellen, then blew her a kiss.

"My Joan of Arc."

Everybody clapped.

Ellen, in fact, looked immobile, immobilized, strangely removed, still as a statue. Her bald head exposed. She looked like she was waiting. Waiting for the firing squad. Waiting for someone to get the pyre together, pour the gasoline, so she could strike the match.

Sammy just looked like a kiwi fruit, and he let his hair grow back quickly.

~

73.

Sammy tended to idolize his mentors, but he also was fickle. No, that wasn't the right word. That word sounded stupid. It sounded like something to do with a soap opera romance, or like a new ice cream treat advertised at the commercial break. Sammy was changeable. Disloyal? No. Quirky. Really, she didn't know what Sammy was.

He had idolized Alex, until he died, and before that he had idolized Walt, until Walt seemed to shrink. He idolized Seth Greenough, but Seth had gone, finally, away. When Sara and Peter kicked Seth out for not doing his chores Seth had still hung around the neighborhood, until his enlistment. He was a visible presence because he actually was living in the Greenough garage. They'd kicked him out, but not too far.

Sammy would go over to the garage, and he reported that Seth had boarded up the side door from the garage that led to the house. Seth had to go out the big garage door and in through the front door for meals. Sammy, until recently, had been more in the habit of divulging. He divulged that Seth had set up a hammock, which Sammy thought was cool, and he divulged that Seth had a black light, and a little mini fridge, and he divulged that Seth had posters of chicks with big boobs and no clothes on. She nearly choked on her Cheerios when Sammy said that, but she tried to maintain a non-judgmental response; she tried to make an observation, rather than shriek. So she said, "Women's bodies are beautiful."

But were they? Really? She had to ask the hard questions. (She, ok, really, truthfully, down deep, thought women's bodies were funny. Funny-odd, funny-strange, forget fun, they weren't supposed to be "fun," she wanted to say to Sammy, if a woman's body was fun, she wanted to say, then *run*.) The hard answers to the hard questions usually came down to one. Women's bodies were human, like any other body. Mortal, mainly. Temporary constructions that could topple in a blink.

And she felt that, in turn, at any moment she could maim Sammy beyond belief. Stunt him, cripple him with her thoughtless words. But she wanted to achieve honesty, honesty in all her relationships, a phrase that, itself, rang with dishonesty. "All her relationships." Who were all these people she was supposed to be having relationships with? There was Dirk. And there was Sammy.

~

74.

There were 1. Responsibilities, and 2. Options. Dirk was laying it all out, even though she and Dirk had agreed they would stage a mini-argument about military service, which would then morph into a conversational exchange. Dirk was going to be pro-military, or at least "pro" the concept of military service, and she was going to be anti-military, keeping it one step short of WIM. She knew that if she aligned the "anti" stance with Sara Greeley-Greenough—dressing in black every first Tuesday of the month and keening down on the bridge with the other Women in Mourning, the WIM women—Sammy would completely tune out or else view the whole scenario of military service, compulsory or not, as along the lines of Halloween.

She had put some thought into her approach. She was simply going to pull up some statistics—how many years Vietnam had been going when they reached the 2,000 body count, how many years it kept on going after that, how many 58,000+ bodies there finally were, and that's just the Americans, the young American boys, barely out of high school, still making their plans, or having no plans, just caught, swept up, carried away, disappeared, name on a wall.

Etc.

But Dirk dumped the game plan, the mini-argument, or he forgot, who knew, and he already was well into the civic component and the private component, and was getting himself all confused about which of life's activities fit into what, and Sammy was already getting down from his kitchen stool with an eye to the door. She tried to give Dirk a signal of some sort, she kicked him under the table, which achieved little, so she had to make the "T" time-out sign with her hands, which stopped him up short.

"What?" Dirk said.

"You know," she said.

"What??" Dirk said.

"What we were going to do." She murmured this in an undertone, as if she could keep Sammy, two feet away, from hearing.

Dirk gave her his blank face. Then he gave her his baffled face.

"What we were talking about *earlier*," her voice became quiet and she lightly sang the words, her eyebrows raised. "That we *said* . . . we would do-*hoo*." She tried to sound offhand, even affectionate. (Dirk was so DENSE.)

"What??" Dirk said. He offered her his final face, both blank and baffled.

"What we were talking about earlier that we said we were going to do *later!*" she snapped. The whole thing was blown, they'd lost their chance. Sammy was quickly shrugging on his hoodie.

"Which is NOW." She growled the word, sounding like a devil woman, even to her own ears. Not a temptress, exactly. More like that little girl in *The Exorcist*.

Sammy looked alarmed, genuinely; his settled-and-cool face became dislodged for a second and his intrigued-but-wary face flashed. Then it turned red.

Then—"I'm outta here!" he said, spinning on his heel. And he was gone.

Dirk's face stayed the same.

~

75.

The funeral was Catholic and the burial was military. Father Flynn from Christ the Redeemer intoned a few words of Latin over the casket, graveside, a special request from Coach Murphy. Dwayne, who'd been raised Presbyterian, was pissed, but no one was listening to him. He had sent his only beloved son to his death. Apparently it was one thing for God to do it, quite another if you were Dwayne. That—despite the neighborhood's initial approval of Alex's patriotism, and more than a little pride and excitement at their association with his "tour of duty," a phrase they liked to use and repeat to each other, as if Alex were a rock star—was the current sentiment and the likely conclusion. It was Dwayne's fault. Blame it on Dwayne.

Requiem aeternam, Dona ei, Domine, said Father Flynn. *Eternal rest grant unto him, O Lord*. He translated for the Presbyterians, sprinkling holy water on the flag-draped coffin.

Alex was inside it.

Et lux perpetua luceat ei.

And let perpetual light shine upon him.

Everyone sat very quietly in the folding chairs set up on canvas flooring laid over the autumn grass. There was a brief bit of singing, a long, wobbly "A-a-a-men," but hardly anyone could get a sound out. At the church service the Senior Girls' Triple Trio from Alex's

high school had sung the old hippy song, *Turn, Turn, Turn*. They'd
worked it up for the Sixties Night concert, so had it fresh. Father
Flynn allowed this, because it was in the Bible, too.

For every thing . . . (turn, turn, turn). There is a season . . . (turn, turn, turn).
They swayed slightly as they sang and allowed their long hair to
drape over their eyes so they could shake it back into place.

Flowered boxes of Kleenex, provided by Discovery Memorial
Gardens, passed up and down the rows. Down in the valley a train
called, singing their sorrow for them.

Requiescat in pace. May he rest in peace.

Amen.

Dirk stood with the other pallbearers, his eyebrows in the rigid,
raised position that she recognized as his precursor to crying. She
stood between Sammy and her father. Sammy was dry-eyed, but
he was shivering, even though the day was warm. He wore one of
Dirk's dress shirts, the long tails left out. He'd grabbed a tie at the
last minute and had it tied around his neck in a granny knot. He'd
slapped away her hand when she tried to fix it.

Walt stood on the other side of Sammy. He kept his baseball cap
on, brim backwards. He wore a t-shirt that said Porn Star, most
inappropriate, though she knew it was a skate brand. The Kleenex
boxes were making the rounds. Walt was the only person audibly
crying in her immediate vicinity. He couldn't stop. He made an
odd, coughing sound when he cried, as if he were choking. It was an
embarrassing noise, and she knew he must feel mortified that all the
doleful, dewy-eyed girls in the row of folding chairs directly behind
them could hear it. Sammy patted Walt on his skinny shoulders,
hesitantly, a kind of confused encouragement.

Guns were fired into the sky, making her father jump. Their
echo reverberated for a bit, then disappeared into a deep hole of
silence. She looked up and saw a jet trail slowly spinning its way

across the sky, the thin white line starting out sharp and neat, then becoming blurred. The guns fired again, and the flag was folded. Celeste accepted it for Ellen, who looked straight ahead and didn't move.

Her father had driven the three hundred miles from his place to theirs, a frightening thought. He was past the age for highway driving, but he'd consulted no one, he just showed up, an hour before the funeral, his legs unsteady from all that sitting behind the wheel. Now he leaned forward and grabbed the folding chair before him with both hands, as if he were still going somewhere, or getting ready.

She and Sammy touched fingers, their arms at their sides, their fingers hidden in Sammy's long shirt. Occasionally one or the other of them murmured something profane, "Fuck this," for example, or simply, "Shit." They whispered it very softly, so only they could hear.

~

VII.

THE LIGHTS

76.

She still had on her acrylic gloves. She sat in her rocker and
rocked. She still had on her corduroy coat and pink beret. Outside
it was just dark. She looked at the rose lamp but didn't turn it on.
Outside it was Halloween.

When she came home she had found her door unlocked. The
Welcome mat was crooked and the key was gone. The yellow comforter
was on the floor. Her scarves were rumpled, slight indentations visible, a bit of oil on the silks, marks the size of a finger. A smell, too,
sweet and tarry and stale.

She clutched her satchel. She had tried to warn the house, the
house of the boy. Everyone outside, looking up the tree, looking up
at the little dog, flung there, a cruel taunt, a threat, a whim. She had
tried to warn the house, her house, the house that was invaded. She had
tried to save it, save the boy, offer a signal, a sign. She had circled back
and looked for an opening, and found it from a side yard, a side door,
she had entered the kitchen and from there found her green glade of
peace, the living room with its magazines, the candle, the chair.

But the clock had chimed, the body had been reclaimed, the
people of the house turned back, towards her, just standing there.
She saw them through the window, but they couldn't see her. Not
then, not yet. And she had panicked, retreated, abandoned them,
she fled.

Inside her satchel was another gift for the boy, a gift undelivered. It was a plastic coin purse that gaped open when squeezed, a silent mouth. The words "State Farm Insurance" were printed on the red plastic in gold letters. Inside the purse were three quarters and a tiny box of Chiclets and a spelling word—imminent *adj*: ready to take place: about to occur. . . . *in ~ danger of being run over.*

And there was a necklace—an image on a chain, a man with a staff. She had found it inside the pocket of a Christmas sweater, itself found at Secret Treasure. The sweater had snowflakes and reindeer and a cozy cottage with smoke curling from the chimney and "Mr. and Mrs. Claus" on a sign hanging from the cottage. The man with the staff was holding a boy on his shoulders, carrying him securely.

~

She opened the bottle of lighter fluid and turned in a slow circle, turned and turned, drawing larger and larger arcs in the shag carpet and up the wall until the bottle was empty and she began with another, turning, turning.

She stood still, then, her body moving slightly, in rhythm with her heart. *One aw-loo, two aw-loo, three . . .*

She sat in her rocker, holding the matches, feeling the beat of the blood in her vessels and her veins. A peace, descending. A wordless dream, rising. Solitary, delicate, clear.

She opened the silver packet and struck the first match, flinging it across the room. Match after match, they sailed through the air, heads aflame, soldiers and kings! The fire burned quickly. It was hot and clean and bright.

~

77.

Sometimes she and Eddy went back out, her breath coming in puffs, Eddy's in a thin, smoky stream from the mouth hole of his mask. Their own house was empty, the others were full. They warmed back up and went back out, looking for lights. The lights on the porches flicked off, one by one, and, by ten o'clock, most of the lights were gone. They walked silently down the streets then. They just drifted.

ACKNOWLEDGMENTS

Deirdre McNamer, Kate Gadbow, and John Carter each helped this book in important ways. Bryan Di Salvatore extended all sorts of writing encouragement, early on. And from the very first contact with Diane Goettel I've felt in good hands with Black Lawrence Press.

Final touches and a lot of reflection happened at the Virginia Center for the Creative Arts, where my residency was funded by the L.E.A.W. Foundation, with assistance from the Montana Arts Council.

The quote in Section V. (The River) comes from *In the River Sweet* by Patricia Henley, originally published by Anchor Books and used with permission from Penguin Random House. Permission to quote from *Owl Moon*, by Jane Yolen, also comes from Penguin Random House.

My thanks go to all.

Photo: Willy Carter

Megan McNamer grew up in northern Montana and studied music at the University of Montana and ethnomusicology at the University of Washington. *Children and Lunatics* is her first novel. She lives in Missoula, Montana.